forever FOUR

· leading ladies ·

GROSSET & DUNLAP
Published by the Penguin Group
Penguin Group (USA) Inc., 375 Hudson Street,
New York, New York 10014, USA
Penguin Group (Canada), 90 Eglinton Avenue East, Suite 700,
Toronto, Ontario M4P 2Y3, Canada
(a division of Pearson Penguin Canada Inc.)
Penguin Books Ltd., 80 Strand, London WC2R 0RL, England
Penguin Group Ireland, 25 St. Stephen's Green, Dublin 2, Ireland
(a division of Penguin Books Ltd.)
Penguin Group (Australia), 250 Camberwell Road, Camberwell,
Victoria 3124, Australia
(a division of Pearson Australia Group Pty. Ltd.)
Penguin Books India Pvt. Ltd., 11 Community Centre,
Panchsheel Park, New Delhi—110 017, India
Penguin Group (NZ), 67 Apollo Drive, Rosedale,
Auckland 0632, New Zealand
(a division of Pearson New Zealand Ltd.)
Penguin Books (South Africa) (Pty.) Ltd., 24 Sturdee Avenue,
Rosebank, Johannesburg 2196, South Africa

Penguin Books Ltd., Registered Offices:
80 Strand, London WC2R 0RL, England

Text copyright © 2012 by Elizabeth Cody Kimmel. Illustrations
copyright © 2012 by Penguin Group (USA) Inc. All rights reserved. Published
by Grosset & Dunlap, a division of Penguin Young Readers Group,
345 Hudson Street, New York, New York 10014. GROSSET & DUNLAP
is a trademark of Penguin Group (USA) Inc. Printed in the U.S.A.

Library of Congress Cataloging-in-Publication Data is available.

ISBN 978-0-448-45549-5 (pbk)   10 9 8 7 6 5 4 3 2 1
ISBN 978-0-448-45613-3 (hc)   10 9 8 7 6 5 4 3 2 1

forever FOUR

· leading ladies ·

by Elizabeth Cody Kimmel
Grosset & Dunlap
An Imprint of Penguin Group (USA) Inc.

For friends: Marnie, Shelagh, Terry,
plus me makes FOUR

· chapter ·
1

"Of course they're staring. We're famous now, ya'll, remember?"

I rolled my eyes at my friend Tally, but at the same time, I couldn't help looking around to see if she was right. And she was. Everyone in the cafeteria really *was* staring at *us*.

"Maybe they're staring because you've got a piece of toilet paper stuck to the back of your pants," Ivy suggested, her pale-blue eyes glinting with fun.

As Tally squirmed around in her seat to get a better look at her backside, Ivy caught my eye and winked. I grinned back at her.

"Nobody is staring, and there's nothing stuck to your pants," Miko said, tucking a strand of her long, glossy, black hair behind one ear.

Miko sounded like she was in a bad mood, which came as no surprise. She'd been acting out of sorts for days. In fact, the last time I could remember seeing Miko smile was at our victory ice-cream celebration five days earlier.

The four of us had had a lot to celebrate that night. We had just won a middle-school competition to fund our own magazine, *4 Girls*. At first, none of us had been thrilled to learn that the principal wanted us to work together on the project. We were a strange group: a mysterious New Girl (Ivy, who's now my best friend), a Drama Queen (Tally, getting more dramatic by the minute), Miko (Queen of the Prom-Queens-in-Training), and regular old me. It seemed like we had almost nothing in common, but somehow the combination of our personalities was *magical*. The first issue of *4 Girls* was so good that we won the competition and enough funding to do more issues for the rest of the school year. Every four weeks we'd get to tell the other students what was most important to them. It was *so* cool.

Now the whole school was talking about *4 Girls* and about the four of us. In a way, Tally was right— on the day our very first issue came out, we sort of turned into instant celebrities.

But we'd barely had a chance to let it all sink in when Miko told us she might not be able to continue working on the magazine. She said it was because she had too much homework and a National Honors project coming due on top of everything else. I knew Miko had a lot on her plate and that her parents were really hard on her about academic stuff. But the thought of our star designer leaving *4 Girls* practically gave me a panic attack. Could three girls handle the work of four?

Well, she hasn't quit yet, I thought, crossing my fingers under the table. Maybe it would help if I could show Miko that we weren't going to have the same kind of superstressed, down-to-the-wire rush to finish this issue. We knew what we were doing now—we were Pros.

"So listen, I'm caught up on all my class work, and I'm totally ready to jump into issue number two," I said enthusiastically. "I mean, seriously, you guys. You can really count on me to do whatever it takes."

"Great, Paulie," Ivy said. "In that case, do you think you might be able to swing by my house and do a little vacuuming? And maybe some light dusting while you're at it?"

I stuck my tongue out at her.

"That is *soooo* sweet of you, Paulina," said Tally earnestly, pulling her mane of wild, blond curls loose from a faded, purple cloth elastic. "Because I for one am going absolutely nuts. Did y'all know the auditions for *Annie* are only a week away? The waiting is killing me. I swear, I don't know how they expect any of us to function!"

"Wait, this is you *functioning*?" Ivy asked. "Okay, I definitely don't want to be around when you're not functioning."

"Oh, no one does," Tally said cheerfully.

On top of being a Drama Queen, Tally was a world-class space cadet, and she knew it. But she never minded when someone kidded her about it. That was one of the many things I really liked about her.

"Anyway, guys, we need to get down to business," Ivy said. "Everyone's read the e-mail I sent last night, right? Are we pretty clear on what each of us needs to do?"

"Wait, which e-mail?" Tally asked.

I rolled my eyes and tossed a grape at her, then snuck a peek at Miko. She was pushing some pasta salad around on her plate, a frown clouding her perfect features.

"The e-mail confirming the topics we're covering for the next issue, like Homecoming? And the auditions and rehearsals for *Annie*? Ring a bell?" I asked.

Tally gave a little squeal of delight. "We're doing the issue on *Annie*? What a *great* idea!"

"It was *your* idea, Einstein," Ivy said. "And we're not doing the whole issue on *Annie*. Just a feature. You and Paulie are doing that part. Miko and I will handle Homecoming Week, which will give us plenty of material. Did you even skim my e-mail, Tally?"

Tally looked genuinely confused now. "Which e-mail?" she asked again.

I sighed.

"Boy, I'm glad it's Friday," I said.

"Is it Friday today? Yay, it's Friday!" Tally exclaimed.

Ivy smacked her hand to her forehead. "Oh, now I've got that awful song stuck in my head," she groaned.

"Oh, you mean the one that goes *Friday, Friday, yesterday was Thursday, tomorrow is Saturday. . . ,*" Tally sang.

"Stop it," Miko said sharply.

Tally's voice abruptly broke off. She looked at me and Ivy. "What did I do?" she mouthed.

I shrugged, then looked back at Miko. Something about the look on her face gave me a bad feeling. The feeling she was about to quit then and there.

"So we're all good, right?" I asked hopefully.

Miko bit her lip, not meeting my eye.

"Look . . . ," she began.

No!

"Like I said, now that we know what we're doing, the next issue really won't be as much—"

"Look," Miko interrupted. "I'm sorry, Paulina. It's nothing personal or whatever. But I can't do this. I told you guys last week I might not be able to. It's just—between my extra credit stuff and violin lessons, I'm stressed out enough—but this National Honors project is due four weeks from today. I just don't have time for anything else."

"What do you mean?" Tally asked.

"She's quitting," Ivy said, the irritation clear in her voice.

Ivy and Miko weren't all that crazy about each other to start with. After our big win last week, I had thought they were starting to get along a little, but they were still far from being friends.

"I think Miko just means she needs us to step up for her for a little while, which I can totally do," I volunteered. "If I can figure out the design software, I could even—"

"No, Ivy's right," Miko interrupted me. "I'm quitting."

My heart sank. It wasn't like this came as a huge surprise, but I had really been hoping we could avoid it. It was clear to me that the main reason *4 Girls* had been such a success was the combination of *all four* of us. We each brought something totally unique to the group. Without Miko, I was afraid *4 Girls* would fall apart.

My disappointment must have been obvious in my expression. Miko caught my eye for an instant. She almost looked sad. Then she looked away. She stood up, clearing the remains of her lunch.

"I have to go," she muttered.

"Miko, wait," I said. "Listen, I totally understand what you're saying. This is a stressed-out month for you. But please don't quit right *now*. What if we say that you're kind of stepping back for a while—sort of taking a little leave of absence until you get your honors project turned in. The three of us can handle putting this issue together. You wouldn't have to do anything right now except maybe answer a question or two about the design program if I have trouble figuring it out. Then, when your project is finished, we can talk about it again."

Miko looked torn. I could tell she wanted to just quit right now and have it over with. But I needed her to stay in our group, even if we had to work without her this time.

"Please, Miko?" I begged. "Just call it a temporary leave and agree to talk about it again when the timing is better?" I knew I sounded a little pathetic. But right then, I didn't care.

Miko held my gaze for a moment, shifting her weight from one foot to another.

"Okay," she said at last. "A leave of absence, then."

"Great!" I cried. I looked at Ivy. I could tell she didn't *quite* share my enthusiasm over Miko's decision. But I also knew she would back me up either way. "We've already got a clear game plan for the next issue," I continued. "We can handle it no problem, right, guys?"

"Handle what?" Tally asked.

Ivy just shrugged.

"Okay, then," I said, feeling relieved. It wasn't a *perfect* solution. But for now, Good Enough was good enough for me. "We'll be fine."

"This doesn't mean I'm not going to have to end up quitting, anyway," Miko warned.

"I know," I said. *But it's going to be fine*, I told myself.

I knew it was going to be fine because I would *make it* fine. Somehow, at the end of the month, I was going to figure out a way to get Miko back on board 100 percent.

"Anyway, I need to go," Miko said.

Miko stood up and made a beeline for the door, walking so quickly she went right past the table of PQuits where her best friend, Shelby Simpson, was waving to get her attention. Shelby turned and shot me a look that said, "What did you do to her?"

Shelby had never liked me. I used to avoid her and all the PQuits, but now I really didn't care. I *did* care about Miko, though. In the last month, I had even come to consider her a *friend*. At least an Off-the-

Radar kind of friend. When the PQuits were around, she was only nice, not overly friendly. But you had to start somewhere—even with friends. Ivy couldn't stand that Miko was practically embarrassed to be with our group. But I could. I didn't *like* it, but I got it. Most of the time.

"Wait, so is Miko quitting or not?" Tally asked.

"She's not," I said firmly. "She's just taking a break."

"After which she will almost certainly quit, anyway," Ivy said, "and *4 Girls* will become *Formerly 4—*"

"Ivy, cut it out," I said. "There are still four of us, and it's going to stay that way. We just need to work around Miko's schedule for a couple weeks. I'm telling you, she'll be back."

Ivy began to peel a banana.

"It's nice that you believe in her, Paulie," she said. "But don't get your hopes up."

It was too late for that. My hopes were already *way* UP. We were going to put together an *amazing* second issue, and we were going to get Miko back. If Ivy wanted to be all glass-half-empty about it, that was fine. I was glass-half-full all the way. *Maybe* that's *why we work so well together*, I thought. Which was good, because we did have a lot of work to do.

And I, for one, couldn't wait to get started.

· chapter ·

2

"Go directly to jail," my mother said, pointing a finger at my little brother.

"Is jail open on a Sunday night?" I asked.

"I don't have to go to jail," Kevin announced triumphantly. "I have a Get Out of Jail Free card!"

"You *always* have a Get Out of Jail Free card," I said.

Kevin was only ten years old, but he was a master at Monopoly. He had a huge pile of multicolored money in a disorganized stack on the table, while I was down to a few measly twenties and tens. And don't even get me started on the hotels he had on Park Place and Boardwalk, *and* the fact that he owned all the railroads and most of the utility companies. The kid was like a miniature Donald Trump. Frankly, it scared me.

"Your turn, sweetie," my mother said, handing me the dice.

"What's the point?" I grumbled as I gave them a

roll. I always grumbled during Monopoly and Kevin always gloated and my mother was always relentlessly cheerful. But really, I loved our Sunday night board game tradition. Plus, I'd get Kevin back next week when it was Trivial Pursuit night. *Nobody* could beat me at that game.

"Six," I said, reading the dice. "So let's see, I go one, two, three . . ."

"You're landing on Park Place!" Kevin exclaimed. "That's mine! *And* I have a hotel, so you owe me fifteen hundred dollars. Ha! Pay up, Paulie!"

I picked up my pile of money and started to count the bills. "I've got . . . sixty. How about a loan?"

"No way!" Kevin declared. "Loans are for suckers!"

"Your sister is not a sucker," my mother said.

"But I *am* bankrupt," I said. "Mom? Can you float me some cash?"

"I've got six hundred and fifty," she said, handing it all to me.

"That's not enough!" Kevin proclaimed. Funny how he was terrible at math unless he was counting Monopoly money. Then he had no trouble figuring out that sixty plus six hundred fifty was NOT fifteen hundred.

"Looks like you win, spaz," I said.

Kevin leaped to his feet and fist-pumped. "I rule the world!" he shouted.

"Always the *gracious* winner, right, Kev?" I said, grinning. "It's fine with me. I need to go check my e-mail, anyway."

"Don't stay on the computer too long," my mother said. "It's getting late, and tomorrow is a school day."

My mother, Psychologist Extraordinaire, had a theory that staring at a computer screen right before sleeping activated some eyeball-to-brain function that gave a person disturbing dreams. It was her own special variation on the wait-a-half-hour-after-eating-before-swimming thing.

"I won't," I promised. "I'm kind of beat, anyway."

"Because I *beat* you," Kevin gloated.

"You'll get yours next week, midget," I said. "And don't forget—winner cleans up the game. Which means sorting the money and putting it back in order."

Kevin stared at the mess in front of him. The thrill of victory started to fade as he considered the task. "But I'm the winner," he complained. "I should get something out of it."

"Virtue is its own reward," my mother stated.

"Enjoy your reward," I said, grinning as I stood up and walked out of the living room.

• • • • • • •

Upstairs, I flopped comfortably on my bed and opened my laptop. There was a massively long e-mail from my friend Evelyn with a link to a bunch of pictures. Evelyn had moved away over the summer and was now bombarding me with pictures and videos documenting every aspect of her new life. I'd save that one for later—Evelyn would want a highly detailed reply and a complete essay on each and every picture she'd sent. I knew she was having a hard time adjusting. That's why she was so eager for my attention. I was more than happy to give it, but tonight I didn't have time.

I scanned the latest entries on the *4 Girls* blog, which had currently become a debate on the pros and cons of turning the latest must-read book into a movie. I'd learned early on it was best to stay far out of those arguments.

I was surprised no one had answered my e-mail about having a quick *4 Girls* mini status meeting at lunch tomorrow. Actually, Tally didn't answer more than half the time, and since Miko was officially on a leave of absence, I guess that didn't require an e-mail. But Ivy was the most organized person I'd ever met. She never let details slip through the cracks.

"Maybe she's as exhausted as I am," I said. I shut down the computer and put it on my desk.

I crawled under the covers, mentally going over the stuff I wanted to bring up at our meeting. I knew the second issue was going to be great—with its real look behind the scenes of the Drama Club's big fall production.

And if Tally ends up being cast as Annie, all the better, I thought. We'd have an exclusive with the star of the show. An insider's look!

I could hear Kevin singing his weird version of the theme from *Star Wars* down the hall. I was allowed to stay up an hour later than he was, but tonight I didn't want to. I was happy just lying there running different versions of the new cover through my head.

4 Girls had brought a lot of surprises to my life, not the least of which was actually looking forward to a Monday morning at school.

· chapter ·

3

Tally Janeway added a whole new dimension to the word *Drama*.

Take now, for example.

Our mini-meeting at lunch on Monday was supposed to be a quick and easy way for us to check in with each other about our assignments for the magazine. Ivy had suggested we have one every two or three days. But lunch was almost halfway over, and I was the only one who had shown up. Until now. Tally appeared at the other end of the lunchroom, surrounded by her usual explosion of chaos. I heard the sound of a lunch tray hitting the floor, followed by a shriek.

"Oh my goodness, y'all, I am *so* sorry!"

Tally had collided with an eighth-grader and knocked the tray out of his hands. She stood there staring at him, her blue eyes enormous. The tray lay on the floor by her feet, with a scattering of tater tots, a heap of broccoli, and two hot dogs that had both popped out of their buns. One lone tater tot was clinging to the front of Tally's sweater. A ripple of laughter was beginning to spread through the cafeteria. It looked like every student in the entire school was enjoying the scene.

"That was *totally* my fault," Tally exclaimed. She crouched down and started piling the spilled food back onto the tray. Her collision victim watched for a moment, then turned and pulled a face at a bunch of his friends who were howling with laughter at a nearby table.

"I didn't see you because I am in *a state of shock*," Tally said loudly as she chased some tater tots across the floor.

The guy shrugged and bolted out the door, leaving his spilled lunch behind. When Tally stood up with his tray, she looked mystified. Then she caught sight of me and headed in my direction. The tater tot still attached to the front of her sweater bobbed up and down as she walked. She did not notice most of the school still watching her and cracking up. Or maybe she just didn't care. I was still amazed by people who could be The Center of Attention (good or bad) and not care.

"Paulina M. Barbosa, you are a sight for soooooore

eyes," Tally sang in her cream-thick southern accent. "You will never believe in a million years what just happened to me."

Oh, what do you bet I would?

Tally placed the tray on the table and plopped down in the chair next to me. "First, I think my school bus temporarily blinked out of time and space this morning," she stated matter-of-factly. Like that kind of thing happens to most people occasionally.

"So the reason I say this," Tally continued, "is because I know for a *fact* that I had my French homework with me when I got on the bus. I was talking to Mary Elizabeth, only she was sitting a few rows up so I had to raise my voice a little because you know how the bus is in the morning—louder than a circus—and I was telling Mary Elizabeth about how toast made in a toaster oven tastes completely different than toast made in a regular toaster, when there was this little *shimmer*."

Tally paused, like she was waiting for me to react.

"Tal, that's very interesting, but lunch is almost over, and we're supposed to be—"

"Exactly!" Tally responded. Which made no sense whatsoever. "It made me lose my train of thought, and I actually *forgot* which kind of toast I like better. Can you imagine? And then when we got to school, my French homework was *not* in my book bag. But it was

17

absolutely, definitely, one hundred percent there when I got on the bus."

"Well . . . maybe you—"

"I know!" Tally said. "That's what I realized. If I had the homework, and then it was gone, there must have been some kind of Bermuda Triangle thing, which is what that shimmer was. The light was being distracted because of the warping of space and time. You know, like when planes and ships disappear because all their instruments go crazy and compasses won't work anymore? My bus must have driven through a place like the Bermuda Triangle and dropped into one of those parallel dimensions where there's a double of each of us and every single thing except they're a little different, and somehow when we popped back, I got the wrong version of my book bag. The one that didn't have my homework in it."

I had to admit, it was an incredibly original and creative explanation for missing homework. The fact that Tally more than possibly believed every word of it was . . . unique.

"Wow," I said. "That's quite a start to a Monday morning. But, Tal, we need to talk *4 Girls*. I have no idea where Ivy is—I haven't seen her at all today. Anyway, you were going to ask the drama teacher if it was okay for us to cover the auditions for *Annie*? And take pictures? Remember, we want to write the review during a dress rehearsal so that it will be in print before the show officially opens. I sent you that permission form for the principal. Twice. Did you get it?"

Tally blinked at me a few times like I'd just switched languages and was now speaking in Swedish. Then she reached into the back pocket of her jeans and pulled out a piece of paper that had been folded into a tiny rectangle.

"I got it," she said. "And I got the principal's and Ms. Whelan's signatures."

Wow. With Tally slipping in and out of time and space, I was amazed that she'd not only printed out the form but gotten it signed.

"This is great," I said, taking the form. I unfolded it and tried to smooth out the creases. "So I'm going to write the main article about *Annie* from auditions to opening night. We'll cap it off with a review of the show. You should focus on writing a piece that's from an insider's point of view—like a diary of your experience or an interview with someone. When are the actual auditions again?"

Tally let out an enormous sigh.

"This Friday," she said. "*Five days* that I have to endure Valerie Teale prancing around, bragging how her voice coach is going to get her a three octave range so she can hit all the notes in 'Maybe.' That girl really—"

"Is there anything going on before auditions that I can sit in on to get material for the article?" I interrupted. "I'd love to get a feel for what you guys are doing and how the Drama Club operates."

"We're having audition workshops every day after school," Tally said. "Starting today. So people can run lines and practice singing with the pianist while certain people brag about their vocal coach repeatedly until I go stark raving mad and am taken away by the guys in white coats to one of those padded rooms all wrapped up in a stray jacket."

"I think they call them straitjackets," I said with a small smile. Tally lived for the theater. It was already bringing out a competitive side I'd never seen before—this issue would be so much better than the last! "Audition workshops—that will be perfect! I'll come watch, and that will give me a feel for who's who and how you guys work and what's coming next."

"What's coming next is my hands around Valerie Teale's smug little neck," Tally declared.

"Well, that would certainly add an exciting dimension to my article," I said, taking a bite of my sandwich. "'Murder in the Theater'—an exposé, by Paulina M. Barbosa." I smiled, but Tally seemed to be contemplating an actual murder. "Don't worry," I said. "I'm sure your audition is going to be great.

You'll take out Valerie with your acting skills—not your assassin skills."

Before Tally could respond, there was a burst of laughter from the biggest table in the lunchroom. I didn't even need to look to know it had come from the PQuit table—territory of the Prom-Queens-in Training. I couldn't help glancing over at Miko. She was putting something in her bag, which was hanging from the back of her chair. As usual, she looked perfectly put together, like a team of stylists had swooped in to work on her between classes. She was so pretty, but these days her delicate features were pulled down in a scowl most of the time. Her gaze met mine as another burst of laughter came from her friends. Miko looked away as if she hadn't noticed me at all.

She just feels bad, I told myself. *A little guilty, maybe.*

"So, anyway, Tal, are you clear on what you need to do? Can you decide over the next couple of days what your *Annie* piece will be?"

"Oh, sure," Tally said. "But how will we deal with the art and design stuff—all the things Miko is good at?"

"We'll figure it out," I said. "If we sort of stick with the same layout Miko came up with for the first issue and we pick something easy for the cover instead of creating original art like she did, we should be able to handle it."

"I could never do this if you and Ivy weren't in charge," Tally said. "You guys are so organized, it's scary."

I laughed a little. I didn't *feel* organized half the time, but I guess compared to Tally . . . then I thought about Ivy again. Where *was* she, anyway? We usually talked and texted a bunch of times during the weekend even if we weren't getting together.

She must be out sick, I thought. *I bet she got clobbered by that superflu.*

Tally reached for one of the tater tots on the tray. It was halfway to her mouth before I exclaimed, "Tal, don't! That was on the floor!"

She froze, then put the nugget of deep-fried potato back on the tray. "Oh yeah," she said. "I can't believe I plowed into that guy like that."

"You actually have another one on your . . ." I pointed to the front of Tally's sweater, where the tater tot was still hanging on for dear life. A nugget-shaped survivor.

"Oopsie," Tally said, pulling it off and holding it out to examine it. "Wow! It's Abraham Lincoln!"

So much of what came out of Tally's mouth seemed crazy that her remark barely registered. But when she turned the bit of potato toward me I had to admit it really did bear a remarkable resemblance to Honest Abe—beard, hat, and all. I was about to suggest she try selling it online when she popped it into her mouth.

"Delicious," she said.

I shook my head. "You're nuts," I told her. "And why were you telling that guy you were in a state of shock, anyway? Did something happen?"

Tally gasped and smacked her head with one hand. She leaped to her feet, almost knocking her chair over, and without another word she dashed out of the cafeteria leaving me alone and bewildered.

Like I said. The girl added a whole new dimension to the word *Drama*.

· chapter ·
4

The school nurse usually posted the list of students who were out sick after lunch. I ran to check it before my next class, and yep, Ivy's name was there. During study hall, my last class of the day, I sent her a quick text telling her to call when she felt better. If I got caught texting I could easily get detention, but there was a substitute teacher acting as warden today, so people were quietly breaking the rules. I took advantage of the situation to send Evelyn a little e-mail, too. A "can't talk now, but miss you, more soon" kind of thing, but it was something.

After the last bell rang, I went to the auditorium. I was excited and intrigued to be sitting in on the first day of audition workshops. Like most students, I always showed up for Drama Club productions. Last year's showcase of *The Sound of Music* had really wowed me, with huge, painted flats that slid in and out to change scenes, gorgeous costumes for the von Trapps hand sewn by someone's mother, and a breakout performance by a guy named Bart, who'd been cast as Baron von Trapp. Now, here it all was happening right around me. I'd never gotten so much as a peek behind the scenes, and I was psyched to have an official *4 Girls* reason to spy. There seemed to be a circus of activity in every corner, and people were milling about, huddled in little groups or stretched out with their feet up on the seats. All at once I heard the sound of enthusiastic clapping.

Tally's friend Buster Hallowell had climbed to the top of a ladder set up on the stage. He was perched on the second to top step, about fifteen feet in the air, holding on to the ladder with one hand as he leaned in the opposite direction. His hand stretched toward a purple sweater dangling from a pipe hung over the stage.

"Buster, you're going to break your neck!" Tally yelled. She was standing in the center of the crowd, clutching her friend Audriana Bingley by the arm. The rest of the crowd showed their approval with wild hoots and applause.

"You've almost got it," Audriana called. Tally smacked her on the shoulder.

"Don't encourage him!" she shouted.

"Who *encouraged* Martin to throw it up there

25

in the first place?" Audriana retorted. "I need my sweater back!"

Near the edge of the stage, a girl wrapped in a scarlet muffler and wearing matching fingerless gloves stood with her hands on her hips, a disapproving look on her pale face. Her lips were moving, but it wasn't until the clapping died down that I could hear what she was saying.

"—can strain your vocal cords," she said. "My coach says never to shout, not even if there's a fire or a disaster. Save your voice and let someone else do the yelling."

Valerie Teale. Of course. Note to self: Do not stand next to this girl during an emergency.

"Buster, come on," Tally cried even louder. "Get down off there!"

His fingers were not more than a half inch from reaching the sweater. He leaned out a little farther, and I felt a sick feeling in my stomach.

He really is going to fall, I thought. *And it's going to be bad.*

"Buster!" Tally squealed.

In a quick movement, Buster reached forward and swung his hand out. Before I could even catch my breath, he was climbing down the ladder like a monkey, the purple sweater clutched in his hand and a triumphant smile on his face.

Buster tossed the sweater to Audriana. Then he made a deep and lengthy bow to the still-applauding onlookers.

"In the footsteps of the Great Farini and the Flying Wallendas, I give you the Hovering Hallowell!" Buster declared, pointing to himself and bowing again.

He froze midbow, his gaze at the back of the auditorium. Tally and Audriana turned to look at what Buster was focused on. The whole crowd instantly fell silent as if they'd all simultaneously received the same direction.

I turned to see what had gotten everyone's attention.

A man was striding down the center aisle. He was slender, with a thick shock of jet-black hair and little, round glasses perched on his long nose. He wore jeans and a dark-gray turtleneck, a navy-blue sweater draped over his shoulders. As he swept past me I got a slight whiff of cologne—the scent a mixture of oranges and nutmeg. He climbed up the little stairs on the right side of the stage. At the same time, the students all filed off the stage on the opposite staircase, again as if they'd received a telepathic command. By the time the man reached center stage, they were all sitting quietly in the first few rows of seats. Even Tally was silent and at attention.

"Good afternoon," the man said, his voice deep like a pleasant rumble.

"I am Gideon Barrymore. In the theater"—he paused here to let the word *theater* sink in—"there are no secrets. So some of you may already have heard that your drama teacher, Ms. Whelan, has unexpectedly had to vacate her position to attend to a pressing personal matter."

I could see Tally nudging Buster and nodding wildly. I guess that explained the State of Shock Tally had been in at lunch. Ms. Whelan was like the center of the Bixby Middle School theater universe.

"As luck would have it, I have just finished an engagement in Manhattan, and as a personal favor to Ms. Whelan, I'm very pleased to be stepping in for her in the great tradition of all understudies who come unexpectedly to the fore in the commitment to an age-old adage—quite simply, the show must go on."

There was a buzz of excitement rippling through the auditorium at the mention of New York. Tally was leaning forward in her seat, watching intently as if Brad Pitt himself had just descended to the stage on a fluffy cloud of golden glory.

"Know this," Mr. Barrymore continued, "in the theater there are no levels of distinction, no most important versus least important. I have seen performances in remote hamlets such as your own that rival any I have witnessed on Broadway. As such,

I will be treating each of you not as students, but as peers and equals. I will not coddle you or give you any greater or lesser courtesy than I would show any veteran of stage and screen. I consider us all professionals here, and I have great expectations that this showcase of *Annie* will rank among the most memorable that this little school has ever known."

Wait! The disappearance of Ms. Whelan and the pep talk by her last-minute replacement would be perfect for the article! I fumbled in my bag, feeling around for my *4 Girls* notebook, but it wasn't there. Feeling panicked that I was letting good material slip away, I grabbed my cell phone, addressed a text message to myself, and began typing some snippets of Gideon Barrymore's remarks.

"I presume you have all brought the audition sides that Ms. Whelan distributed, since actors must always come prepared. I'm going to pass around a clipboard, and I want each person to write their name, contact information, and three—yes, I said three—parts in *Annie* that you would be interested in playing. We will—"

I was glad Mr. Barrymore paused. I was typing on the tiny keyboard as fast as humanly possible, and I was still back on the part about him being fresh off the big stage in New York.

"Excuse me? You—what is your name?"

I was almost done now. Just a few more sentences.

"There are certain offenses I simply will *not* tolerate in the theater."

Part of my brain registered that somebody was about to get in trouble for something. Bummer for them. I just needed to finish one sentence, then hit send.

"Put that thing down!" Gideon Barrymore barked.

I had that sudden, awful moment where I realized that somebody was definitely in big trouble. And that somebody was ME.

I looked up. Sure enough, Mr. Barrymore was glaring at me—his eyes blazing. I could feel that every person in the room was looking at me, too. My hand opened, and my cell phone clattered to the floor.

"That is the first and last time anyone gets a free pass for using a cell phone in my theater. Are we all absolutely clear about that?"

Everybody seemed completely clear. I was about to throw up I was so embarrassed. There was no way I could try to explain right now. I tried not to cringe, waiting to see if he was going to yell at me some more.

But it was like a shark attack when a great white suddenly turns and swims away after just one bite. Mr. Barrymore went straight back to business, asking for a volunteer to walk the clipboard around. I was left in my seat with a big bite taken out of me, and my cell phone possibly broken at my feet. I was too scared to check, let alone breathe.

I sat there for the next fifteen minutes, silent and still, while the students who planned to audition filled out their forms. I was afraid if I got up to leave, Mr. Barrymore would notice me and have something else to be outraged about. Nobody came over to talk to me, not even Tally. I couldn't blame her—I'm sure she wanted to make a good impression on Gideon Barrymore, and she wasn't going to do that by associating herself with a Rude and Offensive Cell Phone User like me.

"That is all for today," Mr. Barrymore said finally. "When we reconvene here tomorrow after school, we will begin the audition workshop. I expect each of you to be prepared—know your lines, understand the character you're reading for—give me *depth*."

With that, Mr. Barrymore turned on his heel and walked down the stairs two steps at a time. Then, in an encore performance of his entrance, he strode up the aisle and disappeared through the door at the back of the auditorium.

In under two seconds, Tally was standing over me.

"Isn't he amazing? Paulina, does he hate you now? Will he ever forgive you? Will you ever forgive *yourself?* How amazing that he was in a show on Broadway! I'm so excited! Do you feel like you're going to *die?*"

I didn't answer any of Tally's questions—I don't think she ever really expected people to. Audriana appeared behind Tally and grabbed her arm.

"What parts did you sign up for? I can't believe he made us pick three!" Audriana said. She had put her purple sweater back on. Her light-brown hair had been recently cut and hung in a perfectly straight line just at her chin. Her bangs were flawlessly even. Audriana always seemed to be thought out in advance, organized. The opposite of Tally, in other words.

I picked my phone up and shoved it in my bag, not checking to see if it was broken or not. My priority was getting out the door. I had just had more than enough of The Theater for one day.

"Annie, Miss Hannigan, and Grace Farrell," Tally was saying. "What parts did you put down?"

"Annie, Miss Hannigan, and Grace Farrell," Audriana replied.

"Why did you put down Annie, Aud? You don't want the lead."

"I don't know," Audriana said with a shrug. She looked a little taken aback by Tally's comment, but Tally didn't seem to notice. "I just did. I've got nothing to lose by auditioning for it."

"You'd be perfect for Miss Hannigan," Tally declared. "You're so great at comedy—you're the perfect sidekick!"

"I don't know . . . I get tired of being the sidekick," Audriana said.

Tally squeezed Audriana's arm. "You're hilarious," she said. "Just what a leading lady needs standing beside her."

Audriana looked like she wasn't so sure she wanted to BE hilarious anymore. I wondered if changing roles in the theater was as hard as changing roles in life. Sometimes I wished I could still be the Girl Unnoticed that I'd been with Evelyn instead of one of The Four like I'd become since we'd launched the magazine. It had been hard . . . but good, too, I think. *Maybe Audriana is ready for that, too*, I thought. *The hard, but good.*

"My mother is picking me up," I told them. "I should go."

"Did you hear Valerie Teale talking about that stupid voice coach again?" Tally asked, apparently not even hearing me.

"She probably made the whole thing up," Audriana replied.

Figuring they wouldn't miss me since they weren't even listening to what I was saying, I left them to their exchange and slipped out the side door. I cut across the playground and doubled back toward the parking area where my mother was supposed to meet me. I scanned the lot for her car, muttering to myself when I couldn't find it. I've tried everything I can think of to get rid of this embarrassing talking-to-myself habit, but nothing works. Midmutter, I realized someone was standing beside me.

Oh great. It was Mr. Barrymore. I don't think he heard me or even saw me. He was rummaging around in a beat-up-looking briefcase kind-of-a-thing as he walked. I could probably avoid him altogether by bending down to tie my shoe or pretending to be on my phone. Then I remembered our first Phone Incident and vetoed that idea.

This is ridiculous, I told myself. *If I'm going to write about* Annie, *I can't be terrified of the director.*

"Mr. Barrymore?" I said.

He looked up, startled. Then he saw me standing beside him.

"Hi, sorry to—I'm Paulina . . . I was in your—I'm the one who—"

He pointed at me. "The one with the cell phone," he said.

It's funny—he seemed larger than life when he was up onstage. But face-to-face, he wasn't that much taller than me.

"I just wanted to apologize about that. Not that I'm making excuses, and I certainly won't do it again, but I was actually making notes on what you were saying and texting them to myself for an article for my magazine."

He squinted, narrowing his eyes that seemed more gray than blue.

"Magazine?" he asked.

"Yes, a school magazine—a student-run thing. We have a blog, too. It's called *4 Girls*. We do a new issue every four weeks, and I had gotten the okay from Ms. Whelan to write about *Annie* for this month's feature. I'm supposed to attend your dress rehearsal so the review will be printed in time for opening night, but then I realized—"

"Excellent," Mr. Barrymore said. The lenses on his little, round glasses reflected the sun, making him momentarily look like he was shooting light beams out of his eyes. "And you want to interview me for the piece?"

"Oh. Well, actually that could be an interesting—"

Mr. Barrymore produced a business card, seemingly out of midair, and handed it to me.

"I'd be more than happy. I always have time for my friends in the press. You can e-mail me here, and we'll set something up." He walked off briskly, humming to himself.

I could see my mother's blue Toyota pulling into the parking lot, but suddenly I couldn't move.

Wow. I had just scored an interview with the director without even trying!

I was definitely getting good at this reporter thing.

· chapter ·

5

"Yes, Sensei Joe!"

The sound of a crowd of ten-year-olds shouting at their karate teacher was almost more than my ears could handle. My little brother's class was running late, and somehow I'd gotten stuck tagging along with my mother to pick him up. Tuesdays were always busy, and sometimes I ended up wherever Kevin was. I hated to miss Day Two of the audition workshop, but I'd be back again for Day Three tomorrow. I rubbed my temples, feeling a headache coming on, and wondered how my mother could look so incredibly cheerful in the midst of all the shouting.

"Roundhouse kick!" commanded Sensei Joe. "With power and focus!"

The kids lined up, many of them hopping from one foot to the other in anticipation. In their soft helmets, mouth guards, and neck-to-knee padding, they looked like an army of hyperactive Pillsbury Doughboys. I wondered, not for the first time, how wise it really was to pay good money to teach Kevin how to attack something with his feet.

I turned my attention to the little screen on my phone. Tally had e-mailed a link to Gideon Barrymore's website, and I was staring at a tiny photograph of the man himself. The bio read:

> Gideon Barrymore lives and works in Manhattan, where his recent stage credits include *A Midsummer Night's Dream, The Seagull,* and *Rosencrantz and Guildenstern Are Dead.* In addition to his Broadway work, he has made numerous film and television appearances, including his award-winning portrayal of Sergeant Dodge Maven in *Corn People III: Revenge of the Colonel* and an upcoming guest spot on the season premiere of the Emmy-nominated sci-fi drama *Nebula Wars.*

I forwarded the link to Ivy. She'd been out again today—I wondered if she had the flu that was going around school. I'd been able to keep on top of *4 Girls* stuff for now but wanted to keep her in the loop.

And I thought that since she'd moved here from New York City just a few months ago, maybe she'd heard of Gideon Barrymore. Maybe she'd even seen him in a show.

Another e-mail from Tally popped into my box.

▼ **To: Paulina M. Barbosa**
▼ **From: StarQuality**
Subject: !!!

OMG, NEBULA WRS IS ON THIS 2MORRO NITE U R TuTALLY INVOTED OVER 2 WiTCH WITH ME!!!

That actually might be interesting, I thought. I had never been to Tally's house, and I was sort of curious. Was her family half as nuts as she was? What if they were *twice* as nuts?

"Mom, watch! Mom! Paulie! Watch!"

I looked up at the sound of my brother's voice, which was audible even over the digital dance music always blasting at the dojo. When he saw that both Mom and I were looking, he aimed a wild kick at his target—a blue, plastic ball on a string hanging from a contraption that looked like a fishing rod, which was being held by one of Sensei Joe's many assistants.

"*Eeeeeeeeyah!*" Kevin screeched. He leaped forward as he kicked, which I'm pretty sure he wasn't supposed to do. His foot connected with the ball, the fishing rod thing, and the assistant, in that order. Both Kevin and the assistant ended up on their backs on the mat. Kevin jumped to his feet, pumped a small fist in the air, and shouted, "Yes!"

No points for style, but I had to give my little brother props for enthusiasm, so I clapped loudly. My mother stuck two fingers in her mouth and made a shrill, high whistle. Kevin ran to the back of the line, but before he could get a second shot at glory, Sensei Joe announced that class was over for the day.

"Did you see me? Did you see my kick?" Kevin demanded as he ran up to us. I tried to guide him toward the door with my mother. The usual crush of kids leaving was colliding with students coming in for the next class, and the doorway was blocked by a woman struggling with a large, redheaded boy who appeared to be permanently trapped in his own helmet.

"You were the spitting image of Jackie Mason," my mother assured Kevin as we waited for them to move out of the doorway.

"I think you mean Jackie Chan, Mom," I corrected.

"Did you see it, Paulie?" Kevin pressed.

"I saw it," I assured my brother, pulling him around the obstacle to follow our mother out the door. "It was very . . . *kick*tastic."

"Kicktastic!" Kevin yelled in agreement. I tried to

get him to move down the street toward the car, but he kept stopping to aim random kicks and chops in the air.

"Hey, have you ever heard of Gideon Barrymore? He's an actor in this movie *Corn People III: Revenge of the Colonel*?" I asked.

Kevin came to a sudden stop, and he smacked his head with his hand.

"*Everybody's* heard of that movie!" he told me.

"Have you actually seen it, though?" I asked.

"Are you kidding? It's like the greatest *Corn People* movie ever made." Kevin looked at me and rolled his eyes. I bet he was thinking, "Big Sisters" the same way I was thinking, "Little Brothers."

"What about the actor? He was in *Nebula Wars*, too," I continued.

"*Nebula Wars* rocks," Kevin confirmed. "Death to the Techutrons! Report to command base! All systems on vaporize!"

Wow. Two for two on Gideon Barrymore's work. Even if Kevin didn't know the guy by name, his enthusiasm for the shows made Gideon Barrymore a certified celebrity, at least in my house.

"How about *Rosencrantz and Guildenstern Are Dead*?" I asked as we reached the car.

"Haven't seen it, but it sounds way cool," he said. "Can you hold this?"

Something plastic and wet plopped into my hand. Kevin's mouth guard.

"Kevin, gross!" I yelled.

My mother hovered by the driver's door, searching for her keys. "What's wrong, Paulie?"

"He handed me his mouth guard," I exclaimed. "It is so disgusting. Seriously—I'm going to throw up!"

As soon as the locks clicked up, Kevin yanked open his door, got into the car, and buckled his seat belt, an innocent expression on his face. My mother came around to where I was still standing on the sidewalk, holding the mouth guard as far from my body as I could. She took it from my hand, neatly wrapped it in a tissue, and dropped it into her purse.

"Thank you." I sighed.

"Anytime," she replied.

I climbed into the backseat next to Kevin.

"Next time I'm going to cream that guy," he announced over the sound of the car starting.

"That's great, Kev," my mother said, squinting into the rearview mirror as she pulled the car onto the street.

"Really?" Kevin asked eagerly.

"Tally asked if I could come over tomorrow night," I said.

"Tally? That's nice, honey—you've never been to her house, have you? But why on a Wednesday night?

Wouldn't the weekend be better?"

"Mom, really?" Kevin repeated. "When I kick, does my foot go higher than my head?"

"It's for *4 Girls*," I said. "Stuff for the next article. Believe it or not—the director of *Annie*? The new theater instructor? He's going to be on this TV show tomorrow night, and Tally wants me to watch it with her."

"Mom, does it?" Kevin pressed.

"Sounds like fun, Paulina. Just make sure your homework is done first," she added. "Kevin, your foot does go higher than your head when you kick, and I just don't know how you can do it. Doesn't it hurt?" A few spatters of drizzle fell on the windshield, and she switched on the wipers.

"Oh yeah, it kills!" Kevin confirmed, grinning proudly.

"I actually kind of like Tally," I said.

"Is Tally the one with the hair or the one with the girly clothes?" Kevin asked.

Ivy was my only friend that Kevin acknowledged by name, since she had proven herself worthy by being a *Battlestar Galactica* fan. Tally and Miko, who had been to my house several times when we were working on the first *4 Girls* issue, he simply called The Hair and Girly Clothes.

"The Hair," I said. "Girly Clothes is kind of taking

a break from *4 Girls* at the moment."

"Bummer," Kevin said.

Word.

"Oh, honey, Miko didn't change her mind about that?" my mother asked. "That's really too bad. How will you get the design and the layout done without her?"

Why did everyone keep asking me that?

"I'm sure that after a couple weeks off, Miko will be back," I said. "And if I have some problems with the design program, I can just ask her. It's not like she's moving to Siberia. I've got everything covered."

"I'm sure that you do," my mother said encouragingly.

I nodded in agreement. Paulina M. Barbosa: Poster Child for the Power of Positive Thinking.

"No, really, I'm fine," Ivy said, closing her locker, then opening it again and staring inside like she'd forgotten something. "I just feel like I was out for more than two days—today doesn't feel like a Wednesday."

"I know," I said. "Isn't it really weird when you're convinced it's like noon, and it's actually only ten, and then you find out someone else thought the *EXACT* same thing? Like, couldn't it be possible that time actually does slow down sometimes, and we just don't know it?"

"Uh-huh," Ivy said, still staring into her locker.

"Ivy? Are you sure you're okay?"

She turned and gave me a slightly startled look.

"What? Yeah, I'm totally fine. I just zoned out there for a second."

"Trying to find out what it's like to be Tally Janeway?" I asked with a grin.

"Oh *please*," Ivy said. "You'll give me a relapse, and I'm weak to start with. Hey, look at the time—we should get going."

Ivy looked like her normal self, dressed in her usual vintage clothes—superfaded jeans and a green, men's dinner jacket that set off her cranberry-red hair. But she was still a bit pale and tired looking from the epic flu that was going around. I sure hoped I didn't get it.

"Hey, listen, I came up with an idea for how to deal with the cover art situation," I said as we walked down the hall.

"Yeah?" Ivy asked. "I'm sorry. I said I was going to figure that out."

"Um, you were practically dying, remember? Anyway, I came up with something easy. Since we can't do original art like Miko made for the first issue, I was thinking how about a photograph instead? What if we just take a picture from the back of the auditorium—of empty seats and a bare stage. It totally sets up one of our features, following the Drama Club from the very beginning of casting to their first dress rehearsal during tech week."

Ivy nodded.

"That's a good idea," she said. "It will be easy to do, saves us a bunch of work, *and* it will look great."

I beamed. Of the four of us, Ivy was the closest we had to a professional when it came to magazine work. When Ivy lived in New York City, her mother had been an editor at a huge magazine. Some of her know-how had definitely rubbed off on Ivy. She had a great sense of what would work and what wouldn't.

"And I've got a good digital camera," Ivy added. "So I'll take care of getting the picture."

"Awesome," I said. "Oh, and Monday at the mini-meeting I got the signed permission form back from Tally, and—oh, I haven't even told you about *The Actor* yet!" I pronounced it with exaggeration: *ak-torr*. I'd already started to think of Mr. Barrymore as The Ak-Torr.

"What *ak-torr*?" Ivy asked. Her third-period class was on a different floor than mine, so there wasn't much time for me to bring her up to date.

"There's a new drama teacher! Ms. Whelan apparently had to leave, no one knows why, and this guy shows up to take her place, and he's this real actor from New York. You should have seen him yesterday, Ivy—he gets up onstage and he's like, 'Hello. I am Gideon Barrymore.'"

"Weird," Ivy said.

"Weird?" I asked. "How come?"

"Just that, you know—the Barrymores are about the most famous family of stage actors on the planet. Kind of funny that a Barrymore would show up at a tiny school way upstate to take over a middle-school production of *Annie*."

Huh. I didn't think of that. "I didn't realize Barrymore was a famous theater name," I said. "So you're saying it's weird that an actor would leave New York City to come up to a tiny town no one's ever heard of? You should tell him you're from the city, too! You can bond over the bagels and the skyscrapers and all the stuff you miss!"

Ivy paused at the stairwell, shaking her head.

"But I *don't* miss it," Ivy said. "Why do people assume that the city is automatically *better*—that if you had the choice, you'd rather be there?"

"I don't," I said, giving Ivy a funny look. Something seemed . . . different. And not flu symptom different. "I like it here."

"Right?" Ivy asked. "Me too. Who knew at the ripe old age of thirteen I'd find out I'd been a small-town girl all along? If—"

The rest of her sentence was drowned out by the sound of the first bell, which was especially deafening in the stairwell.

"I've got to run and so do you," I said, hoisting my bag over one shoulder. We had four minutes to get to class before the late bell rang.

"Okay, catch you later," Ivy said as she headed for the stairs.

I went back into the hall. My social studies classroom was just a few doors down. A small group of girls was standing by the student announcements bulletin board, tacking up a huge poster for Homecoming Week.

Where there was a planning committee for a dance, there were PQuits. Miko was one of the mightiest of all the PQuits, and she was standing right in the center of the group, a stack of posters under her arm. She looked glamorous and professional in black skinny jeans and a matching turtleneck, her glossy, dark hair pulled up in a twist.

I couldn't help but wonder. How did Miko have time to be helping with dance stuff if she had zero time for *4 Girls*? I felt a little flame of resentment.

Be fair, I told myself. Miko was different with her PQuit friends than she was when she was with me and Tally and Ivy. They put a lot of pressure on her to follow the group. Miko had never been quite comfortable with her two different worlds—I never knew if she would be friendly or aloof to me when her friends were around.

I decided I'd be friendly first.

"Hi, Miko," I replied. "How's it going?"

"Oh," Miko answered. She looked flustered to see me. "It's going okay."

"Did you design that?" I asked, pointing to the poster in Miko's hand.

I didn't mean for it to sound like an accusation, but Miko held the poster partly behind her back, like she didn't want me looking at it.

"It only took a few minutes," Miko replied.

Shelby had been pulling things off the bulletin board to make room for the poster. Now she turned around and saw me. She rolled her eyes, like I was someone's irritating little sister trying to muscle in on what the big girls were doing.

"They're for Homecoming," Shelby said. "We are totally blowing last year's theme out of the water."

Another one of my mother's Psychologist Specials is that the key to being friendly is showing interest in what someone else is doing. It's kind of scary how often it works. Ivy and Shelby couldn't stand each other, so if I could get some inside Homecoming info right from the horse's mouth, I knew Ivy would appreciate it.

"I heard about that," I said. "It's kind of a time travel theme, right?"

"No," Shelby said. "It's decades. Each grade is assigned one. The eighth-graders get to pick, so they snapped up the sixties. Sixth grade is the eighties."

Like I said. Kind of a time travel theme.

"So what decade will the seventh-graders be?" I asked.

Miko had gone back to tacking the poster up. Shelby stared at me, her hand on one hip, but the look of impatience was partly gone.

"The seventies," she said. "Which will be way fun. Everyone is supposed to dress in their decade style on Decade Day. Whatever class has the most participation and the best outfit wins the School Spirit Award. And I'm making it my personal business to make sure that the seventh grade wins. The winning grade gets an entire homework-free day. Every teacher has to agree."

"That sounds really cool," I said, going for the old butter-her-up thing.

"I know," Shelby said. "I'm completely psyched. Take one of these flyers and pass the word."

Then she actually smiled at me as I took the flyer from her.

Score another one for Mom Psychologist.

"So, we're actually doing some stuff on Homecoming for the next *4 Girls* issue," I said. "It would be really fun to have pictures of people from every grade—like a 'best of' thing. Everyone would *love* it." I knew I was laying it on thick, but I also knew that when dealing with PQuits, you had One Chance to get it right. If Shelby dismissed me with a PQuit glare, me, Ivy, and our *4 Girls* article were done for.

"Maybe," Shelby said. "I'll talk to my people and let you know."

She would *talk* to her *people*? This was Homecoming, not the Golden Globes.

But Shelby had already lost interest in me. She examined the placement of the poster Miko had hung.

"It needs a border," Shelby said. "Something to make it pop—maybe pink or orange."

"In your dreams," Miko said. "It's done. And this is the way it's supposed to look."

"But, Meeky, it's got to make a splash," Shelby protested. "We talked about this at the Dance Committee meeting, remember?"

I felt another flash of irritation. Miko found the time to go to one of Shelby's Dance Committee meetings? That didn't seem too important. Or stress-inducing. Actually, it sounded a lot like . . . hanging out with her best friends.

Maybe I've been wrong about Miko all along, I thought.

I turned and walked away. And I wasn't really surprised that *none* of the PQuits noticed.

• • • • • • •

I walked into social studies just ahead of the teacher, Ms. Zangeist, and slid into my usual seat in the second row. I had just enough time to notice that Benny Novak was in the seat next to mine before Ms. Zangeist launched into a speech about carpetbaggers and Reconstruction. I felt a very small flutter in my stomach.

Last year I had been completely unable to function whenever Benny was around. This year I'd come a long way. We actually had regular conversations now. And he even played the occasional prank on me. Nothing too involved—your basic fake spider in the locker kind of thing. But I would definitely say we were *friends*.

Benny was looking my way, and when I met his eye, he pointed at a flyer on the bulletin board and mouthed, "Homecoming?"

I nodded and twirled my finger in circles by my head while crossing my eyes in a universal symbol for Totally Insane. Anyone who knew me knew that school spirit stuff like going to dances was not exactly my thing.

Ms. Zangeist began passing out some work sheets, and I realized that she was giving us our homework assignment. I yanked the cap off my pen and started scribbling, hoping I hadn't missed anything.

"No less than five pages, typed please, and it needs to cite at least three sources that do not include the textbook and are reputable. That means no Wikipedia!"

I sighed.

The paper was due on the same day I had to give

a book report in English. I circled the date in my homework planner and added a few stars beside it. I'd have to remember to start the book report early if I was going to get both assignments done on time. But I couldn't work on either one today. I had to go to the audition workshop for *Annie* after school and then to Tally's house to watch *Nebula Wars*.

"If you have any questions or concerns, now is the time to speak up," Ms. Zangeist was saying. "You all know I don't accept last-minute excuses."

A hand shot up over near the window. I recognized the shiny, gold bracelet. It belonged to Tally's archenemy, Valerie Teale.

"Ms. Zangeist, the due date for the paper falls during tech week for *Annie*. We're going to be having long dress rehearsals that week to get ready to open the showcase. For those of us who have principal roles, will it be possible to get an extension? Because there will be rehearsals every day after school, and some of us have special coaching sessions as well—I need to be able to plan my schedule."

I snuck a look at Tally, two seats behind me. Her normally creamy complexion had turned bright red.

I could see why Tally would be mad. It was totally obnoxious the way Valerie spoke as if she already had the starring role.

"Yes, Valerie, we can certainly discuss that,"

Ms. Zangeist said. "You may see me after class."

"It's only Wednesday, and auditions aren't until Friday," Tally blurted out. "Nobody will know who's getting the leads until Monday at the earliest."

Valerie smiled and nodded, giving Tally a look that seemed to suggest that *she* knew very well who was getting a lead.

· chapter ·
7

"I totally messed up. Can I start again?"

Messing up was putting it lightly. Audriana had started the song okay, but just a few lines in, her voice broke in a disastrous squawk. It sounded like the cry of a goose that had just seen a flash of the butcher's knife.

Mr. Barrymore walked to the front of the auditorium and stared up at Audriana like she was a statue with an extra arm or two feet facing backward.

"We *never* break during an audition," he said. "And we never apologize or make excuses. I need you to get this because we only have today and tomorrow to rehearse before Friday's auditions."

I watched curiously, scribbling a few notes and feeling thankful I did not have to get up on that stage.

"But then what do I do if I mess up?" Audriana asked him.

She stood clutching her sheet music, running one hand through her already neatly combed hair. Today she was dressed head to toe in black—she looked like a ninja, but a safe and perhaps teensy bit ordinary one.

"You continue your audition as if you did nothing wrong," Mr. Barrymore said. "*You* know that you made a mistake. The *director* knows that you made a mistake. But it doesn't help to make a face and apologize. Asking to start over again just calls attention to the fact that something went wrong. Project the energy of confidence. Mistakes happen all the time in the theater. You are a professional. You are flexible. You can recover."

Audriana took a deep breath and held up her sheet music. The accompanist, who was also the assistant librarian, played a few opening chords on the piano.

"*The sun'll come out . . . tomorrow . . . ,*" Audriana sang.

She made no mistakes this time. Her voice was clear and very pretty.

How do people do that? I wondered.

Singing in front of people just seemed so . . . brutal. It was like letting people peek into a part of you that might not be so flattering. Like, how your hair looked in the morning when you first crawled out of bed.

"She's doing great, don't you think?" I whispered

to Tally, who was sitting in front of me.

"She'll do better with a Miss Hannigan song. It's not so much about technique," Tally whispered back.

Huh.

Audriana's *technique* sounded pretty good to me. But I guess I had no basis for judging. You would never see me onstage, let alone singing in front of a crowded auditorium.

Tally half turned in her seat to look at me. "Hey, you're still coming over tonight, right?"

I nodded. There wasn't a known force in the universe that could keep me from watching *Nebula Wars* tonight—and being at Tally's house to do so would just be the icing on the cake. Drama Galore. The kind that had nothing to do with me. My favorite.

"All right," Mr. Barrymore said to Audriana. "You've worked on the singing. But where's the story?"

Audriana looked behind her, like The Story might be lurking there, making rabbit ears behind her head and sticking its tongue out.

Mr. Barrymore continued. "*Why* will the sun come out tomorrow? What's going to happen then? How long has it been since Annie has seen the sun? This is an opening into a character's soul, not a weather report. What was Annie's day like yesterday? Does she say that 'the sun will come out tomorrow' every day of her life, or did something happen to make this day different?"

Audriana seemed riveted by Mr. Barrymore's barrage of questions. Several of the students sitting and watching began leafing noisily through their scripts.

"Don't look for answers in the text," Mr. Barrymore commanded.

The sound of rustling pages stopped abruptly.

Mr. Barrymore climbed the steps up to the stage and stood next to Audriana. He tapped himself on the chest.

"In here. That's where you'll find your answers," he said. "These are the kinds of questions you need to ask yourself about a character *before* you audition. What did Annie have for breakfast? What did she do last night? What's the last thing that made her laugh? How long has she been wearing the same pair of shoes? Each of you will come up with a different set of answers. It doesn't matter what they are. The only things that matter are that you know what *you* think Annie had for breakfast, and that every line you deliver supports the idea of what she had for breakfast."

Audriana looked off into the distance, her eyes narrowed in concentration. She made a C shape with her hand and half lifted it to her mouth.

Egg McMuffin, I thought.

"He's right," I whispered to Tally. "I know what Audriana's thinking!" But Tally didn't respond. Her eyes were closed tight in concentration.

"Moving on," Mr. Barrymore said, consulting the clipboard he held in one hand. "Next up we have a Valerie Teale."

Tally went very still and pretended to be leafing through her pages. But I knew she was intensely focused on Valerie.

Here we go, I thought as Valerie stood up and walked to the stage. She was wearing a variation of Monday's outfit—a lemon-striped scarf was wrapped around her neck over a blue T-shirt. She wore faded jeans layered with bright-yellow leg warmers. She looked like she had a little SpongeBob SquarePants wrapped around each of her calves.

Valerie hit center stage with confidence, turned to face the audience, then gave the accompanist a polite nod. Mr. Barrymore sat in the front row, one hand under his chin, watching Valerie so intently it was like he was trying to make her levitate. She didn't seem thrown by it.

Boy, I thought. *That girl has got confidence.*

The accompanist played a few bars of what even I—the only Non-Theater Person—recognized as the opening notes of Annie's biggest number "Maybe."

Valerie took an enormous breath and opened her mouth to deliver the first note.

"Mayb—"

"Stop!" Mr. Barrymore barked.

Valerie stopped, a look of fear flashing across her face before she regained her calm, poised demeanor.

I looked at Tally. She seemed about ready to jump out of her chair in celebration. Her eyes gleamed and a smile tugged at the corners of her lips. Everyone was on the edge of their seats, waiting to hear what Gideon Barrymore would say to Valerie Teale.

"Why have you picked this moment to sing?" Mr. Barrymore said. "Why do you choose the word *maybe*? Why not *definitely*? What are you unsure of? What did you just see that sparked these memories?"

"A scrap of paper on the floor," Valerie said, squaring her shoulders and looking Mr. Barrymore directly in the eye.

Ah. Confidence. *Someday*, I told myself, *I will have a little of that, too.*

Mr. Barrymore snapped his fingers and pointed at Valerie. "Okay. What's on the paper?"

"Part of an address. And a postage stamp," Valerie replied, without missing a beat.

"Yes, all right. And?"

"And the address is crossed out. It says 'Return to Sender.'"

"This is clear! This is good!" Mr. Barrymore exclaimed. "Take it another step."

"Annie wants to be that envelope," Valerie said. "She's ended up nowhere, and she knows it must all be a mistake. She wants to be returned to her parents. Annie wants to go home."

Valerie and Mr. Barrymore were nodding knowingly at each other like a couple of scientists standing over a groundbreaking discovery. I looked at Tally. Her mouth dropped open in shock. Her eyes filled with dread.

"Okay," Mr. Barrymore continued. "Now don't tell me. Show me. Not when you start singing. I want to see everything you just told me in the moments before you start singing."

I was pretty interested to see how Valerie was going to show Mr. Barrymore that she was half of an envelope with a stamp on it. This was fascinating. I made a note to ask Tally more about an actor's process that night. Maybe we could run a tips column next to my article on *Annie* and Tally's first-person perspective in the magazine.

The end-of-after-school-activities bell rang before Valerie could start singing again. She looked bummed that she couldn't show off a little more.

"All right then, actors. To be continued tomorrow. Nice work today," Mr. Barrymore said.

Tally shot to her feet and leaned down toward the row of seats in front of hers where Audriana and Buster were sitting together. They turned around to look up at her at precisely the same moment.

"Yes!" Buster said.

"No," Audriana countered firmly.

"Okay, y'all, but just listen for a second," Tally implored. "Seriously—I've got a plan!"

Tally often had a plan. They tended to be very wordy and difficult to convey.

"Tal, I'll see you at seven thirty, okay?" I said, giving the back of her denim jacket a little tug.

She gave me a peculiar look. "In the morning?" she asked.

"Tonight," I said, laughing. "*Nebula Wars?*"

Tally clapped her hands together and started to say something. But Buster shushed her and pointed. Mr. Barrymore was standing within earshot.

"Seven thirty," Tally mouthed. "See you then."

• • • • • • •

While the whites were chugging around for their final minute in the dryer, I curled up in an old beanbag chair with my laptop. I typed in the address of the *4 Girls* blog.

There was no real reason for me to sit in our laundry room other than the fact that I loved the smell of fabric softener and the gentle hum of the dryer helped me relax. Plus, Kevin never came down here because he was convinced the room was haunted, which guaranteed me a little peace and quiet.

The screen read: YOU HAVE NINETEEN (19) NEW POSTS.

Wow.

I pulled out half a Twizzler I'd been saving and gnawed on it thoughtfully as I began to read. The first nine posts were a continuation of the back and forth argument going on about what qualified as an actual vampire movie. A random Harry Potter fan had jumped in. I sighed, only half reading them. It was more of the usual: This is best ever/worst ever. I adore/detest this character. The movie is never as good/always better. Someone always started harping on *Twilight* again. The same people saying the same things. What did any of this have to do with *4 Girls*?

But there were a few new posts. I opened one.

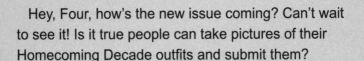

Blogpost: New Issue??
Posted by: SonicSanity99

Hey, Four, how's the new issue coming? Can't wait to see it! Is it true people can take pictures of their Homecoming Decade outfits and submit them?

Oh, great idea, I thought. I typed a quick response.

Re: Blogpost: New Issue??
Posted by: 4Girls

Thanks, SonicSanity99! The new *4 Girls* is coming along great—I'm sure you're going to love it! And absolutely, submit your Decade photos here. And tell your friends!

The subject of photos reminded me of Ivy's shots for the cover. I fired off a quick text reminding her to bring her camera tomorrow and telling her I was going to Tally's to do some research on Gideon Barrymore.

"Paulie? Paulina? Are you down there? *Paulllllliieeee?*"

I sighed and walked to the foot of the basement steps.

"Yes, I'm here, Kevin," I called. "Come on down."

"No way! I'll get possessed and be levitated to another planet. I can't find my green marker. Can you come help me look?"

If I said no or asked him to hang on a few minutes, he'd just stand at the top of the stairs calling my name. I sighed.

"Okay," I called.

"Make sure there's nothing attached to you," Kevin added anxiously. "You might accidentally bring a demon up here."

"Okay," I called again. It was easier just to humor him.

And just to be safe, I gave my jeans a quick check. If I had any demons stuck to me, I couldn't see them.

· chapter ·

8

Tally lived way out on the edge of town. Like Tally herself, the house was adorable on its own but was given a unique look by the bits of extra splash on the outside. The shrubs by the driveway were draped with little orange lights in the shape of chili peppers. A green-and-white flag with a red dragon in the center fluttered above the front door. A roomy-looking tree house was wedged precariously in the V of a huge, old tree in the front yard.

Wow, I thought. *It must have been so cool to grow up here.*

I rang the doorbell while my mother waited in her car to make sure that I got in okay. The door opened, and I took a second to register Tally's outfit—a stiff-looking red dress that looked about two sizes too small, white kneesocks, and a pair of scuffed patent leather shoes.

"I think it's just *stupendous* the way you're always on time for everything," Tally said.

I waved to my mother and followed Tally into the house.

"What can I say—I am known throughout the world for my punctuality," I said.

Tally led me into a small, cluttered living room. It was a room that seemed designed for comfort— huge, mismatched armchairs flanked an overstuffed sofa piled with pillows. Tally flung herself into one of the chairs with a sigh. I noticed she was holding a bedraggled-looking teddy bear, which she clutched to her chest.

"Are you okay?" I asked, taking a seat on the couch. Tally seemed a little out of sorts . . . even for her.

"I am so hungry I could faint dead away," she replied.

"Haven't you eaten?" I asked. "I already had dinner."

"If you can call one tiny bowl of watered-down gruel and a rind of cheese dinner, then I guess I have," Tally responded. "That's all she would give me, and I was lucky to get that much. How I loathe her."

Whoa. What had I walked into? I knew of girls who had terrible relationships with their mothers and lived in a constant state of warfare at home—I just never figured Tally for one of them. But really, I didn't know much at all about Tally other than what I saw at school. I started to feel uncomfortable. Was her mom really that awful? I didn't want to pry . . . but Tally's exhausted tone kind of concerned me.

"Does she know you're still hungry?" I asked quietly. For all I knew, the woman was lurking in the hallway, waiting to pounce.

"Of course she knows," Tally answered. "It's one of the ways she controls me. She is pure evil! I was up before dawn this morning scrubbing out the toilets, and when I was done she called me a lazy, monstrous little creature and told me to scrub them all out again. With bleach! My hands are practically bleeding!"

Now I was really worried.

"This is . . . maybe we could ask my mother how to . . . I mean, can't you explain that the bleach hurt your hands?"

Tally's lower lip quivered, and she stared at me with her huge, blue eyes.

"If I complain . . . ," she began, dropping her voice to a whisper, "I'll be *beaten*."

My mouth dropped. "Your mother . . . beats you?" I whispered.

Tally looked in the direction of the doorway to make sure no one was standing there. Then she leaned in toward me. "Not my mother," she whispered. "Miss Hannigan."

Wait a minute.

Miss Hannigan? Wasn't that the woman in *Annie* who ran the orphanage?

"Um, Tally, are you practicing for auditions right now?"

Tally flopped back in the chair, tucking her feet up under her.

"Not practicing," she said in her normal voice. "*Rehearsing*. It's called method acting. I'm going to completely immerse myself in the character of Annie until auditions on Monday. Every chance I get I'm going to be Annie. Her thoughts are mine. Her *life* is mine. And right now, my frail and bony little body is dangerously close to giving out from sheer exhaustion and starvation!"

Well, *THAT* was a relief. Not the starvation part. The acting part.

"I haven't had a proper meal in months," Tally told me. "I dream about—"

"Darlin', here are your Twinkies," I heard as a box came sailing through the air. Tally leaped out of her chair and caught it.

"Oh yummy. Thanks, Mom."

I turned and saw Tally's mother in the doorway. She looked a lot like Tally, with the same open face and expressive eyes. Her hair was curly, too, but the blond was mixed with gray, and it was cut much shorter. She wore black sweatpants and a striped sweater.

"And you must be the famous Paulina M. Barbosa," Tally's mother said. "Welcome to our crazy house."

"Thanks," I said with a smile. Inside, I was laughing at the idea that mere minutes ago, I believed this woman forced Tally out of bed before sunrise to clean bathrooms on an empty stomach.

A second person appeared in the doorway, an older girl with thick-rimmed glasses and her hair pulled back in a tight ponytail.

"Tallulah, this book is my property, and you cannot violate me by removing it from my desk without my knowledge and treating it with disrespect."

Who is Tallulah? I wondered.

"Paulina, this is Tally's big sister, Marlene," Mrs. Janeway said. Neither of her daughters appeared to hear her.

"I was using it for research," Tally said. "You should be flattered anyone wanted to borrow that boring, old thing."

I could see the title of the book in question: *German Philosophers on the Sisyphean Conundrum of the Poverty Cycle.*

"I am *not* flattered. And you left Cheez-It crumbs in the spine!"

Before Tally could respond, her sister turned and abruptly marched off, taking the book with her. Tally flopped back in her chair and sighed like the weight of the whole world had just lifted off her shoulders.

Mrs. Janeway smiled at me. "You girls enjoy your show and give a shout if you need anything," she said. Then she turned and followed her outraged older daughter down the hall.

"Tallulah and Marlene?" I asked Tally with a grin.

"After Tallulah Bankhead and Marlene Dietrich," Tally said, beaming. "My Dad's a *huge* old movie buff. My sister was plain old Molly until she got to college, but now that she's a philosophy major we all have to call her Marlene."

"I didn't even know you had a sister," I said. "Is she on a break from college?"

Tally shook her head, ripping open the box of Twinkies with enthusiasm.

"Nope, she goes to Hillston U. You know, over in Stipville. She lives here instead of in the dorms. It saves a pile of money."

"That's great," I said.

"No, it isn't," she said. "Oh, four minutes to go!"

Tally dug around the seat cushion frantically, then pulled out a remote and pointed it at the television. As I shifted on the couch to get more comfortable, Tally switched the TV on with one hand while tossing me a Twinkie with the other. The timing was sort of off, and I ended up partially sitting on the little cake and squashing it.

After an embarrassing ad for a shampoo for guys with no hair (Scalp Suds!) and a brief October Chill update from the FlashFive News Team weather specialist, it was time for the main attraction. Tally bounced up and down in her chair and sang along with the theme music.

"Nebula Wars, we will fiiiight . . . on planets of yonder, through black holes of niiiiiight . . . our Techutron foe and their nanoprobe bliiight . . . shall bow to the force of our Rebel-bred miiiiiight . . ."

Tally really had a great voice, though she couldn't sound less like little orphan Annie at the moment. I settled in to watch the show, unwrapping my flattened Twinkie and taking a bite. I had never seen *Nebula Wars* before, so I was sort of lost plot-wise. But I liked the main guy, Commander Saunders, and it was fun that every time a new scene started we looked for Gideon Barrymore. The show was more than half over when Tally shot up out of her seat.

"There he is!" she squealed, pointing at the screen.

All I saw was a quick shot of three men in lab coats. The camera was focused on Commander Saunders and a short, yellow-haired man standing next to him.

"Explain," barked Commander Saunders.

73

The camera panned back to one of the scientists.

"Thuh Gidih Bah!" Tally attempted to exclaim, stumbling over her own words and a mouthful of Twinkie. But she was right. It was him, right there on the screen. He was playing an actual Science Guy in outer space. It is the weirdest feeling ever to see someone you know on TV—it had never happened to me before.

"My sensor readings indicate the presence of nano-tech radiation emissions," Science Guy said.

"In plain English," barked Commander Saunders. Science Guy blinked once before pointing at the short dude.

"Commander, this man is a Techutron!"

The camera zoomed in on Commander Saunders's grim face as the music blared in a Major Plot Twist crescendo. Then the screen went black, and the commercial for the bald-guy shampoo came on again.

"Can you believe it?" Tally shrieked.

"I can't!" I cried. "That was him. Your director! He was really on the show!"

"Did you see the way he blinked?" Tally asked. "Right before he pointed? Isn't he absolutely *amazing*?"

"Commander, this man is a Techutron!" we shouted at the same time.

74

Tally's glee was contagious, and it felt good to laugh until my sides ached.

Science Guy did not make another appearance during the final ten minutes of the show. But Tally and I were still giggling over Mr. Barrymore's performance as the credits rolled.

"Do you think they let him keep the lab coat?" Tally asked.

"Maybe he'll wear it to the workshop tomorrow!" I suggested.

We were still giddy over the show when my mother, even more famous than me for punctuality, arrived at nine on the dot. I saw her headlights turning into Tally's driveway, and felt . . . disappointed. This had been a lot of fun.

"Oh, I've got to go," I said, genuinely wishing I didn't have to. "Can you thank your mom for me?"

"Definitely," Tally said with a grin. "And, Commander . . ."

"This man is a Techutron!" I finished.

I cheerfully endured the usual Mom questions on the short drive back to our house. Did you have a good time? Does Tally have any brothers or sisters? What do her parents do? And the one she always casually sneaks in at the end—how's their house?— which is Mom's way of asking if they are neat or messy.

"I'm glad you had a good time, honey," my mother said, smoothing my dark curls away from my forehead. "It's always nice to make new friends. Oh, that reminds me—Ivy called while you were out."

"She did?" I asked.

"Yeah. She just wanted to let you know she is having trouble finding her camera and the pictures might have to wait another day. And that she'd see you tomorrow."

"Oh," I said. "Okay then."

That's strange, I thought as I went upstairs to change into my pajamas.

I had texted Ivy telling her I was going to Tally's. So why would she call my house if she knew I wasn't going to be home? We usually texted and e-mailed each other constantly, but that had slowed down lately, too. It didn't make much sense. Could I have done something to upset her? Was she mad at me?

Everything had been going so well.

I was suddenly afraid it was all about to change.

· chapter ·

I usually liked Thursdays because all seventh-graders had a free period in the morning. It was a great time to catch up on homework. And we'd had a lot of that lately.

But today something was bothering me. Ivy had never gotten back to me yesterday. I left her a voice mail last night and also sent the whole group a link to a funny post on our blog.

Blogpost: Homecoming
Posted by: MadHatterSpaz

Why do we even have Homecoming? Who is coming home, and where were they before?

It was the kind of thing Ivy usually found hilarious. But she hadn't answered at all. What was even more strange was that we always met at our lockers right before free period, but today she was nowhere to be seen. *What is going on?*

I put my oversize social studies textbook in my locker, then closed it.

"Boo!"

I gave a little exclamation of surprise, something like "Wahooa!" as Benny Novak came suddenly into view.

Benny gave me an apologetic grin. "Sorry. Didn't mean to startle you," he said.

"I'm betting you probably did," I replied with a grin of my own. Not only did he startle me, I felt the old nervous flutter in my stomach again.

"You're actually not that much fun to scare. When I do that to my mom, she usually jumps about a foot into the air and screams."

"Benny Novak, model son," I said.

"I try to stay humble," he said and took a little bow.

"Keep trying," I suggested. "Hey, have you seen Ivy anywhere today? I really need to talk to her."

Benny shook his head. He shifted his weight from one foot to the other, thrusting his hands into the pockets of his varsity jacket. He really was ridiculously good-looking. He'd recently cut his thick, brown hair, but it still had that just-out-of-bed, shaggy look that boys can pull off as adorable.

His eyes were a deep, ocean-blue that made me look twice every time I looked at them.

"So are The Four hard at work on the next Pulitzer Prize–worthy issue?" he asked.

I wasn't telling people that we were currently The Three. I was still determined to somehow get Miko to come back full-time. Then I remembered running into her yesterday while she was "working" with her friends. I had no idea how I was going to convince her that *4 Girls*—and its other three creators—were worthy of her time.

"Yep. I'm doing a feature on *Annie*. Kind of a 'road to opening night' thing. We're going to get a review based on a dress rehearsal so the whole school will have it in time for the opening. Tally's going to do an interview with the director and an insider's perspective, and Ivy's handling Homecoming."

"But you all kind of work on everything together, right?" he asked.

"Oh, definitely," I said. "If this is anything like our first issue, we'll end up having a slumber party and getting everything finished up together at the last minute."

"So you'll probably all be going to *Annie*," Benny suggested. "And Homecoming. Like, even if you normally might not have?"

I saw someone walk down the hallway and instantly

recognized the flash of Ivy's cranberry-colored hair.

"Oh, there she is! I'll catch up with you later, Benny, okay?"

I took off after Ivy before I heard Benny's response. She was moving so quickly, I had to run to catch up with her.

"Hey," I said, coming up behind her.

"Oh, hey, Paulie," Ivy said, not looking at me.

"I was just heading to the library for free period," I said.

"Me too," Ivy replied, adjusting her bag.

Still not looking at me. There was definitely something up.

Neither of us said anything as we walked through the main door into the library. I was so nervous, I had to remind myself to breathe. I hated conflict, and I especially didn't like thinking my new best friend might be mad at me. I didn't know what was going on, but I needed to find out. I would just have to *ask* Ivy—"bite the bullet" as Mom would say.

I looked around for a place to sit. The table by the window was occupied by PQuits. Miko wasn't there, but Shelby was holding court while Daphne and another girl—Kit—listened intently.

"And how about her Facebook wall?" Shelby was saying. "I mean, duh—you're not supposed to 'like' your own status, right? Seriously, who does that?"

Ivy and I both automatically headed for a corner that was several tables away from Shelby but still a safe distance from the librarian's office. This was too important to risk being interrupted in the name of Peace and Quiet. Ivy sat down cross-legged on a rug near the biography stacks, dropping her bag beside her. She chewed on her lower lip, toying with the laces on her boot. There was no doubt about it. She was upset. I sat down next to her and took a deep breath.

"Listen, Ivy, you're my best friend, so I'm just going to come right out and ask you," I began.

Ivy looked up at me, her expression confused.

"I just . . . are you mad at me?"

Ivy looked surprised. "What? No! Of course not," she said. "Why would I be mad at you?"

"I . . . um . . . well," I said. Great. Now I sounded like an Insecure Idiot. "I just felt like there's something going on with you, and I'm worried. I thought maybe I did something to offend you? I mean, how come you waited to call me last night until you knew I wasn't going to be home? You could have gotten me on my cell."

Ivy sighed, fiddling with one of the oversize, silver buttons on her jacket.

"I'm really sorry," she said. "I was being lame. I can't do the cover pictures like I said I would, and for some reason it felt easier to leave a message with your mom than to actually tell you in person. I'm getting a new camera, and I will take the pictures, I promise. Plus, I've been designing this survey for our readers to fill out online, you know, stuff like what worries you, what is important to you. I wanted to turn that information into a pie chart that gives a visual of us as a group. We can call it, like, 'Slice of Middle School Life' or something."

"That's great," I said. "But it isn't *4 Girls* I'm worried about, Ivy. It's *you*. Why won't you tell me what's up?"

Ivy sighed again. "I guess . . . okay, I've been trying to put off telling you this for as long as possible."

Uh. Oh. In the history of the world, no good news has *ever* come after that statement.

"Put what off?" I asked. "Ivy, what is going on?"

"We're moving back to the city," she blurted out.

I stared at her, my mouth open. This was the last thing I had expected.

"What?" I asked. "How is that possible? You just moved here two months ago—school's only just started. How can . . . *why?*"

How can my newest best friend be taken away, just like Evelyn? How can this happen to me *AGAIN*? How will *4 Girls* survive? I added silently.

Ivy pressed her lips together.

"*City Nation* magazine wants my mother to come back to work for them," Ivy said. "They made her some big offer. And all week she and my dad have been having these hushed little talks about it. I was stuck in my room with that bug for two days so I had plenty of time to notice. It was totally obvious what was going on. And yesterday she finally decided to take the job."

"I . . . oh, Ivy. Are you sure?"

Ivy nodded. "She hasn't *officially* told me," she said. "But I know what I heard. She is *definitely* taking the job."

"And she's moving you back to the city? Just like that? She's not going to commute or something?"

"She's definitely not going to commute. It's three hours by car each way. It's a city job—she's a city person. I should have known she'd change her mind eventually and make us move back. I mean, obviously it can't happen right away. They rented out our apartment, so she'll have to find some new place for us to live near her office. All that takes a while. I'm betting when the semester ends for Christmas break is when we'll go. I'm so furious. I feel like I have no power—like I don't count. I left my whole life behind when they decided to move. Now I have to do it again? And the crazy thing is, I really, *really* like it here. And I have you—and *4 Girls*. But apparently that just doesn't matter to her."

"Well, have you said this to her?" I asked. "Because you have to, Ivy. You're a part of the family, not a piece of furniture. You have to explain how this affects your life."

"I can't," Ivy groaned. "Because she hasn't *officially* told me yet. As far as either of my parents know, I have no idea what's going on. I don't exactly want to tell them I was standing there with my ear pressed up against the door when they were talking yesterday."

"Ivy . . . I don't know what to say," I said quietly.

"There's nothing to say," she told me. "Paulie, can we just not . . . I mean, the reason I didn't tell you she got the offer and didn't call you the second I found out we were moving is I just . . . I don't want to talk about it. For right now, for this month or however long it is, I'm still here. I just want to try to enjoy myself—hang out with you, work on *4 Girls*—just like this isn't happening."

I nodded. I wanted to pretend it wasn't happening, too. But it was. All too soon, I'd be without a best friend for the second time in seventh grade.

"I get it," I told Ivy. "For now, it's business as usual."

"Business as usual," Ivy repeated. "Except I've been out of the loop for a couple days. So what is our newest *4 Girls* business?"

"Well," I said. "You should really witness the *Annie*

84

audition workshops, where the drama never stops, even if there's no one onstage."

Ivy grinned, suddenly looking more like her old self.

"Well, now you're talking, Paulina M. Barbosa," she said. "I am definitely looking forward to seeing that."

• • • • • • •

The sign outside the auditorium door was pretty clear.

REMAINING AUDITION WORKSHOPS OPEN TO ACTORS ONLY. THIS MEANS YOU.

"I guess that mean us," I said to Ivy.

As we stood staring at the sign, I heard the tinny sounds of music being channeled through an iPod attached to somebody's ears. I turned around to see Buster coming up behind us wearing scarlet high-tops, orange jeans, and a fire-engine red sweatshirt that screamed MACBETH in gothic lettering. This was not a guy you would lose track of in a crowd.

Buster pulled off his earbuds when he saw Ivy and me standing by the closed door.

"Hey, guys," he said.

"I guess things are getting serious in there," Ivy said, pointing to the sign.

"Oh, you don't know the half of it," Buster exclaimed. "Unless you've talked to Tally recently."

"We were going to meet her here, but apparently we're no longer allowed in," I said. "What's up?"

Buster took an enormous breath and planted both hands on his hips. He did love to deliver a juicy bit of news. "There's a *rumor*," he said, his eyes glinting.

"Annnnnnd . . . ," Ivy prompted.

Buster waited as three eighth-graders walked around us and went into the auditorium. When the door swung shut, he gave me a giddy look, grinning wildly.

"Well, Mr. Barrymore has got all these Manhattan theater connections, right? So apparently Tally heard from someone on Facebook who saw a tweet that somebody apparently retweeted where somebody read an interview GB gave about this play he's directing as a last-minute favor for a friend—which is totally us, right? I mean it has to be—and that it said something about the fact that his agent thought it was a really cool thing for him to be doing and might even come to the show because you never knew where a star might be hiding!"

Buster flung both his hands in the air as he said the word *star* and then gave them a little shake for emphasis.

"So . . . that means . . ." I let my voice trail, hoping Buster would jump in and explain it to me. He did not disappoint.

"An undercover agent is coming to Bixby to, like . . . discover the next Julie Andrews! Or, in my case, the next Nathan Lane!"

"You need tea!" someone was exclaiming. "Tons and tons of boiling hot tea!"

I turned and saw Audriana, who was clinging tightly to Tally's arm, pulling her down the hall toward the auditorium. Tally's face was flushed, and her eyes were red and puffy as if she'd been crying. Or eating something ridiculously spicy.

"Why does Tal need tea?" Buster demanded. "Do I need it, too? Tea for two? For me, for you?"

Buster started to do a little impromptu tap dance, but Audriana reached out and whacked him on the arm.

"It isn't funny," Audriana said. "It's happening again—just like the year we did *Guys and Dolls*. Tal's having a nerve attack."

"Uh-oh . . . ," Buster said.

"A what attack? Is she okay?" I asked. "Tally, are you okay?"

She didn't *seem* okay. For starters, she wasn't answering me. When Tally Janeway had nothing to say, chances were good that something was very, VERY wrong.

"Audie," Buster said. "Tell me the *thing* isn't happening again."

"The thing *is* happening again," Audriana declared.

"I told you to tell me it wasn't!"

"But it is!"

"But—"

"Will someone please tell me and Paulina what's going on?" Ivy interrupted.

No one said anything for a moment. Ivy and I looked back and forth between the three of them.

"When Tal gets superstressed out, she gets . . . laryngitis," Buster finally whispered. "Last time it happened was during costume fittings for *Guys and Dolls*."

"Laryngitis?" I asked.

"It means I can't talk," Tally said miserably.

Well, she could *talk*. But her voice was unusually husky, the way you'd sound right in the middle of a bad cold.

"You do sound a little scratchy," Ivy said. "But it's not *that* bad."

"Not yet," Audriana said. "But if she doesn't turn it around right now, she's going to be voiceless tomorrow during auditions."

Tally made a wretched squeaking sound, and her eyes filled with tears.

"Excuse me," I heard.

Valerie Teale was pushing through our little group to get to the door. Today she was wrapped in a musical-note-decorated muffler. She paused to take in the five of us, tucking a strand of her fine, sand-colored hair behind one ear.

"You all better get in there," she said. "The workshop starts in ten minutes, and you know how important it is to get a good vocal warm-up, right, Tally? How else will Mr. Barrymore know what we can do?"

Valerie tossed one end of her muffler over her shoulder for emphasis, shot Tally a not-so-nice smile, and pushed open the door with her foot before flouncing through.

"Oh, she's so snaky!" Buster exclaimed when the door had closed. "She must be loving *thissss*!"

Tally made another anguished squeaking sound, and Audriana whacked Buster again.

"You'll just make it worse," Audriana scolded him in a stage whisper. "Come on—we've got to get in there."

Audriana pulled the auditorium door open with one hand, steering Tally through with the other.

"Tally, you're going to be fine," I said. "And tea actually sounds like a great idea!"

Buster followed his friends through the door.

"With honey and lemon," I called after Tally. But the door was already swinging shut in my face. Whatever Drama was to come would happen in the auditorium, where Ivy and I were not allowed to go.

At this moment, that was somewhat of a relief.

• • • • • • •

When Ivy ran back to her locker to get her bio notebook, I typed a quick, miserable text message to Evelyn.

> Ev, you're not gonna believe this—IVY is moving away, too. WHAT IS IT WITH ME AND BEST FRIENDS?????????

Moments later the response came.

> Sorry : (Call me later? U R the best!

· chapter ·
10

With the auditions off-limits, Ivy and I both decided to go home and get a jump on our homework. My mom was at the dentist with Kevin, and the house was blissfully quiet, which was great because I'd had a headache all afternoon.

I created a list of everything I needed to do, and I divided it into two columns: schoolwork and *4 Girls*. But my mind kept wandering back to what Ivy had told me. I had the same awful feeling in my stomach that I'd gotten last year when Evelyn told me her family was moving. We had been inseparable for years. I didn't think I'd ever find another friend like Evelyn. And then a new girl showed up at school. Ivy Scanlon.

By Christmas, she'll be gone, I thought. I felt like crying.

I grabbed my phone and hit speed dial number one.

Evelyn picked up on the first ring.

"What happened?" she cried, without wasting time saying hello. "How does someone just up and move like that when they just moved into town in the first place?"

"Her mom got some job," I said, my voice shaky. "Back in the city where they were. I just . . . heading into the first week of school without you was soooo hard, Ev. I was totally miserable. And then I start getting to know Ivy and actually liking her—I mean she's nothing like you—you are totally unique and weird and great and crazy all at the same time, and Ivy's different, but I really like her. And it's just gotten to the point where we're pretty good friends and—"

My voice broke, and I bit my lower lip. I hated to cry. Especially on the phone. At least I could hide it a little.

"I wish I could say something all cheery and full of sunbeams and bunnies," Evelyn said. "But the reality is, this stinks. It's not fair, you don't deserve it, and I feel really, incredibly bad for you."

"Thank you," I said. I never liked it when people instantly took a "look at the bright side" attitude. Evelyn always told it like she saw it, and I loved that.

"Oh no," Evelyn said as a tiny chime became audible. "My mother is texting me. I'm supposed to be clothes shopping with her right now, and I've been hiding."

I laughed. Evelyn and her mother did not share a similar fashion sense. Clothes shopping was always an epic drama.

"Go," I told her. "Listen, text me later or shoot me an e-mail."

"'Kay," Evelyn agreed. I heard her start to call "I said I'm coming!" as she switched her phone off.

Well, now I felt a little better. But I had also just wasted valuable homework time. And my head still hurt.

Focus, I commanded myself. Pick *one* thing on the list. Any *thing*. Then do it.

The outline for the social studies paper then.

Or maybe I'd just quickly get my English reading out of the way? Then I could cross a whole item off my list. But I couldn't remember if I'd written the pages down that we had been assigned.

It's okay, I told myself. Just go to the class page on the school site and look it up. The homework is always posted.

And I did start to do that, but the class website made me think of the *4 Girls* blog, which was getting so many posts these days it was hard to keep up with it. I *loved* reading the blog. I *loved* seeing how we connected with readers and gave girls a place to speak up Every Day.

Just a quick peek, I thought. *Then on to work.*

When I pulled up the page, I gasped. There were six new posts! I thought about coming back to them later, but . . . I opened the first one.

Blogpost: *4 Girls* Issue
Posted by: Galilea7

I have a suggestion for the Homecoming part of the issue. What about doing four big word jumbles, one for each decade of the theme. So for the sixties, you could have words like BELL-BOTTOMS, TIE-DYE, HIPPIES, BEATLES, GROOVY, PEACE, HEADBANDS, SANDALS. For the seventies, it could be PLATFORM SHOES, WIDE TIES, LEISURE SUITS, FEATHERED HAIR, FUNKY, POLYESTER, CHARLIE'S ANGELS, FRYE BOOTS, CLUNKY NECKLACES, and so on . . . you could pick a different kind of print for the word jumble for each decade—like a tie-dyed one for sixties and that fat, plushy kind of type for seventies, maybe rainbow colored?

I loved the idea! It wouldn't even take that much time—Ivy or I could easily design it. I forwarded the link to Ivy to make sure she saw it. Then I hit the RESPOND TO POST key and typed quickly.

I love this! Thanks!

I heard the front door slam and the sound of Kevin talking excitedly. "And they found spider eggs in it, and something that looked like a finger with a bite taken out of it!"

"Kevin, sweetheart, I really don't think that kind of thing happens, even in a fast-food restaurant," my mother was saying, her voice getting louder as she came toward the kitchen.

"No, Mom, it's a true story!" Kevin exclaimed. He walked into the kitchen backward, waving his hands in the air at my mother as she followed him.

"Says who?" she asked.

"Says the Internet!" Kevin shouted. "Right, Paulie?"

"Right," I said, standing up and stretching. "I kind of got distracted this afternoon—was I supposed to be helping with dinner tonight, Mom?"

My mother walked over to me and tucked my hair behind my ears. "No, sweetie, I've got that vegetable chili in the fridge for tonight. Are you okay? You feel a little warm, and you look awfully tired."

I *was* tired, I realized. And my headache definitely seemed worse now.

"I've just been staring at my computer for too long," I said. "That's all."

My mother didn't look convinced. "I hope you're not coming down with something," she said.

"Maybe *I'm* coming down with something," Kevin suggested excitedly. "Mom, if I get a flesh-eating disease, how much school can I miss?"

"You do not have a flesh-eating disease, Kevin," my mother said, turning to open the refrigerator door.

"Or bubonic plague or maybe teet-see-fly," Kevin continued. "I bet you'd have to miss a whole bunch of school for that."

"I don't think the tsetse fly disease is going around right now," I said with a grin.

Kevin looked disappointed.

"Well, it might be," he said. "Maybe we just don't know it yet. Somebody has to go first, right?"

"Somebody has to go make his bed and put his dirty clothes in the hamper since he didn't do it this morning," my mother countered.

Kevin heaved the enormous sigh he reserved especially for the subject of "Making One's Bed."

"I just don't see why I have to when I'm only going to get in it again and mess it up," he said. But he was already halfway to the stairs. Kevin had had this argument with Mom enough times to know he was never going to win.

"You should take a break from that computer," my mother said to me. "Rest your eyes."

"I will," I said, sitting down again. "I just have to finish a few things."

The little voice in my head, the Always Sensible one, urged me to focus on my English assignment. But *4 Girls* stuff was so much more fun. Plus, I had an idea for the first paragraph of my "Road to *Annie*" article, and I didn't want to forget it. Just a few more minutes wouldn't hurt.

I opened a new document. But before I could get my first sentence down, I got distracted again—this time by an e-mail popping into my in-box.

▼ To: Paulina M. Barbosa
▼ From: StarQuality
Subject: : (

My voice is worse, not better, and the audition is less than twenty-four hours away. I am freaking out!! Valerie Teale's Facebook status says "Look out, Annie—here I come," which Molly says is something called passin-agressin. Have you ever heard of it? When my eyes cry, no sound comes out of the rest of me! Also don't kill me, but I don't think I can interview Mr. Barrymore like I promised 'cause I can't even talk, and his undercover agent is coming, which might be what gave me the nerve

attack in the first place, and my whole life could be
ruined if I can't audition, so could somebody else
do the question-asking part for me?

Never a dull moment. I did feel bad for Tally, but I
had to wonder if part of the "nerve attack" was self-
induced. I'd never known Tally to be . . . calm.

I fired back a quick e-mail saying we'd figure
something out and that she should just focus on
resting and trying to get her voice back.

The sound of my own typing seemed strangely
loud. My head throbbed and so did my back and my
legs. As a matter of fact, my entire body ached. And
it was starting to hurt to swallow.

My mother had this strange way of being right
about things before I even knew about them. It
looked like she'd done it again.

· chapter ·
11

Most of Friday was a blur of trying to get comfortable in my bed, eating a little of the hot soup my mother brought me, being too hot and too cold at the same time, and wondering if I was asleep when I was really awake. Finally when I dozed, I had bizarre dreams—like one where I took this huge bite of pie right as Benny Novak asked me a question, and I couldn't say anything back to him because my mouth was full.

On Saturday, I slept—as they say—like the dead. I didn't even wake up until lunchtime. When I opened my eyes, I saw Kevin looming over me.

"Mom says you have a nasty virus," Kevin said, peering down at me like an alien about to experiment on a new human subject. "Can I have some?"

I groaned and pulled the covers over my head.

"Go away," I croaked.

A shaft of sunlight reached my face when Kevin lifted the blanket.

"Take this stick of gum and chew on it a little," he whispered. "Then give it back to me when it's got some good germs stuck in, and I'll chew it."

"Please leave me alone," I groaned.

"Just breathe on me then," Kevin persisted, pushing his face so close to mine he was a blur of freckles and Cap'n Crunch breath.

"Kevin Barbosa, are you in your sister's room?" I heard my mother call.

Kevin bolted from my room.

"No!" he called from the hallway, with the self-righteous outrage of the wrongly accused.

I closed my eyes and tried to go back to sleep, but the damage was done. I was awake.

I lay there like a lobster in a tank, making a little movement every once in a while to make sure I was still alive. Eventually I found the strength to grab the remote from my bedside table, and I switched on the little TV by my bookshelf. I found a station showing a classic movie marathon, and I stared at it while I zoned out. At one point I actually dozed off again.

When I had watched too many movies and consumed enough soup and Flu-Away to satisfy my mother, I switched off the TV, opened my laptop for the first time in two days, and waited for it to start up.

Now that the house was quiet I didn't like it. I didn't like that Miko had left us or that I had to help Tally with her share of the magazine work or that Ivy was leaving me. I hated that. I got a lump in my throat, which hurt a lot because my throat was already sore. I couldn't help but feel sorry for myself. Two days and had one person even thought to call or come see me?

I suddenly remembered my cell phone. The battery was dead. I found the charger and plugged it in next to my lamp.

Finally, my computer booted up, and I logged into my e-mail account. "Hey, I've got e-mail," I murmured. "And Facebook messages."

Two e-mails and a Facebook message were from Evelyn, sending more pictures and a video labeled "Tour of my house and life." My phone buzzed as it came back to life. I had a text, too.

IS IVY STILL MOVING? ARE YOU OKAY?

I owed Evelyn a long e-mail. And a phone call. Maybe even a visit . . . because I definitely did not feel okay.

I turned back to the computer. Four e-mails were from Ivy, ranging from "Are you okay?" to "OMG I just called and your mother told me you have the flu" to "Call me when you're back in the land of the living." A one-line e-mail from Tally said she had not been able to audition. Another e-mail alerted me to a new post on the *4 Girls* blog.

Blogpost: Suggestion Box
Posted by: Tinkabelle

Glad you guys are going to be writing about the Drama Club. Are you going to talk about what it's really like when there's only, like, two or three good parts for girls and all the actresses are going up against each other? To be honest, that's why I've never joined Drama Club. I've heard things can get really nasty. Hope your article will be honest enough to let me in on how true that is.

I wanted to answer before I passed out again.

Re: Blogpost: Suggestion Box
Posted by: 4Girls

Thanks, Tinkabelle, that's a really good point. I've heard the same thing about the pressure being really intense during auditions, but from what I've seen so far, it intensifies friendships just as much as rivalries. I'll definitely give a full report in my article!

Just typing the post was exhausting, like I'd jogged up ten flights of stairs. I lay back on my pillow and relaxed, watching some more of my favorite old movies. By late that night, I was starting to feel a little more like my old self.

I spent what was left of my weekend working on finishing the homework I'd abandoned on Thursday. When I was done, I scrolled through the auditorium pictures Ivy had sent. I loved them and thought there were two or three that would make a great cover image.

"Paulie, you really shouldn't be on your computer anymore," my mother said Sunday night.

I looked up to see her standing in my doorway, holding a tray laden with juice, crackers, something in a bowl, and a teapot with steam wafting from it.

"It was only a little," I said, looking at the tray with interest. This was my favorite part about being sick—the point where I finally started to feel better, but my mom was still fussing over me and bringing me interesting things to eat. She made me feel like royalty.

"Your teachers aren't going to expect your homework to be done when you've been down with such a nasty bug," my mother told me, placing the tray on the table next to my bed.

Ooh, vanilla ice cream!

"I brought you a little of everything," she said as I pounced on the ice cream. "But take it slowly. And I know your inner clock is probably all confused from sleeping during the day, but it's getting late. Focusing on a computer screen at this hour—"

"Will give me disturbing dreams, I know," I said. I closed my laptop with one hand and ate a spoonful of ice cream with the other. "Thanks, Mom."

As usual, she was right. Because when I finally fell asleep that night, I dreamed that it was opening night of *Annie*, and when the lights came up, it was *ME* onstage. I didn't know any of my lines, and instead of having on the *Annie* costume, I was dressed as a giant ham, and Mr. Barrymore was hovering backstage yelling "Something isn't right!" over and over again as the audience laughed their heads off.

And Benny Novak sat in the front row eating vanilla ice cream.

· chapter ·

12

Monday mornings are always a challenge. But when you've had the flu for three days and all you've eaten is soup, toast, and a little ice cream, getting through a Monday can feel like crossing the Sahara Desert. On foot. With no sunblock. And no Gatorade. And a very heavy book bag to drag around.

The only good news was that Ms. Zangeist had apparently come down with the flu herself. And so did Mr. Sadler, the English teacher. I guess it sounds heartless to call that good news, but really—who hasn't secretly celebrated when they learn a teacher is going to be out? Not only were our regular classes canceled, but we were being sent to the library for an extra free period.

I walked to the library by myself. A note had been posted on the door.

Someone tugged at my sleeve. I turned, and there was Tally, with a superlong, striped scarf wrapped around her neck so many times it looked like she was being attacked by a rainbow-colored boa constrictor.

"How's the voice?" I asked, opening the library door and letting Tally go in first.

Tally gave me a sad, little orphan Annie stare and shook her head. She held up a steaming travel mug as further evidence.

"Still gone?" I asked.

Tally nodded, then mimed choking herself, her pink tongue stuck out comically.

Tally claimed one of the small round tables by the window and signaled for me to sit down with her. She reached into her bag and pulled out a large notepad and a fat, orange pen with black pumpkin stripes and a tiny bat on a spring stuck to the end. She scratched a note onto the pad, the bat at the end of the pen bobbing around as she wrote.

Had to audition in sign language. Cast list might be posted today. I'll be lucky to get anything at all.

I made a sympathetic face. Poor Tally. She had been obsessing about getting this part for weeks. She'd even been living Annie in her method acting preparation, wearing that funny undersized, red dress and the shiny patent leather shoes. Now Valerie Teale would probably get the part.

"I'm so sorry. I know what a big deal this was for you," I said sympathetically.

Tally nodded and wrote something else.

It's like a jagged arrow stuck through my soul!

"Oh, Tal. Does it help to remember that there will be other parts and other plays one day?"

Tally gave an enormous sigh, pointed to her heart, then mimed scooping it out of her chest, squishing it between her palms, and hurling it to the ground. She may have lost her voice, but she hadn't lost a single drop of character.

"You know, Tal, this would actually make a really moving aspect to my article," I said. "Do you mind if I mention it? How you worked so hard and then had this laryngitis thing happen at the worst possible time?"

Tally nodded emphatically and gave me a thumbs-up to doubly reinforce her approval of my suggestion. At least she'd be in the *4 Girls* spotlight!

"That would be great," I said. "And listen—I don't know why I didn't think of this myself, but Ivy suggested that you could just e-mail Mr. Barrymore the questions for your interview. That way you don't have to worry about your voice or even deal with him face-to-face. Plus, the answers will come already typed up and everything. That'll save you some work. And I was thinking that instead of just putting it in regular text, we could have some kind of picture of an audience, and the questions could be coming out of their mouths in talk bubbles or something. To make it kind of fun and theatrical. Right?"

Tally nodded and began writing a message to me on her pad. She wrote very slowly.

I waited, trying to be patient. The library was starting to fill up with students from social studies and from Mr. Sadler's English class. Daphne had plopped her bag onto the table right next to mine and was waving Shelby and Miko over. My eyes met Miko's briefly as she pulled up a chair, but she looked away without really acknowledging me. That was fine—I was still irritated by Miko being on the stupid Dance Committee with the rest of the PQuits.

Tally shoved the notebook at me.

Since I have no lines to learn, been doing research, trying to find out name of GB's agent. If I get name, I can Google Image him and find out what he looks like, then I can spot him in the audience! Maybe I could audition for him then!!!!!

"Wow, look at you—you're turning into a regulation investigative reporter!" I said.

Tally's face brightened—clearly she liked the sound of that.

I saw Ivy come in the main library door. She headed for our table as soon as she caught sight of us. She looked a little more like herself today—wearing peg-legged cargo pants and a vintage bomber jacket. There was just a tiny bit of puffiness around her eyes. Only someone who knew her really well might think she was a little bit distracted.

"You made it," Ivy said. "I can't believe you're here—you sounded like death on toast on the phone last night. You had it so much worse than me."

I laughed hoarsely. "I'm still kind of out of it, but I was going nuts cooped up in my room for three days," I said. "And Kevin kept sneaking in trying to trick me into infecting him."

Ivy chuckled. "Was he successful?"

"He was as healthy as an ox this morning," I said. "He was absolutely furious. Hey, any word from your mom on what's going on?"

"They still haven't officially told me," Ivy said, her expression darkening. "They know I'm going to go through the roof. They're acting like everything is all normal, which is really irritating me—they even talked about getting season lift tickets to Ski Wyndham—like they're actually going to do that. I cannot even express how angry I am at them."

"I'm really sorry," I said, silently adding that I, too, could not express the level of anger I had at Ivy's parents for handing her to me like a gift, then snatching her away.

"Tally, how's the voice?" Ivy asked.

Tally wrote GONE in huge letters in her notebook and held it about a foot in front of Ivy's face.

"What a drag," Ivy said, scooching back in her chair slightly. "Are you sure you don't have this bug Paulie and I had?"

Tally shook her head and wrote:

Larringitis from worrying.

"But the auditions were Friday, right? So shouldn't the worrying part be over?" Ivy asked.

Tally scribbled some more.

Not until cast list goes up.

Tally was pointing at her notebook with one hand and making a little "talkity-talk" gesture with the other, her fingers opening and closing like a mouth.

"What does that mean?" Ivy asked. "Does she want someone to draw a lobster?"

Tally made an exasperated face and pushed the notebook toward me, pointing at the thing she'd written about Gideon Barrymore.

"Oh, I think I know what she wants," I said. Tally gave a sharp sigh of relief. Not being able to talk must be agonizing for someone like Tally, who usually spat out thousands of words a minute.

"Tally is trying to find out what Gideon Barrymore's agent looks like, so if her voice is back when he shows up, she can sing a song and recite a soliloquy for him," I said. "So he can discover her."

Tally clapped and nodded way too enthusiastically, like Anne Sullivan when she was trying to teach Helen Keller to say *water*.

"All she has to do is get his name and find his picture," I said. "But she hasn't been able to find anything yet."

"Mysterious," Ivy said. "And speaking of mysterious, Paulie, Benny Novak has made two swoops past this table in the last four minutes."

"What? Really?" I asked. I usually had a pretty sophisticated Benny radar. "Now where is he?"

"Lurking behind the new fiction stack," Ivy said.

"Just ignore him," I said. "He's probably trying to pull a prank. His new joy in life is sneaking up on me and scaring me half to death. Last week he put two rubber mice in my book bag."

All three of us fell silent for a moment. I tried to scan the library for signs of Benny without appearing to do so. I was determined not to be startled into making a squeal like I had at my locker the other day. Bits of conversation from the next table, now growing a little louder, drifted over.

"But that's the whole point," came Shelby's voice. "We're just going to have to do double the work in half the time—we'll be better organized than them on Decade Day. Posters, flyers, e-mail blasts. We should have a Facebook page for it. Somebody should be tweeting. It's only a few days away, people."

"Yeah, well, sorry, Shel, but I don't agree," Miko responded. "It's Decade Day and Homecoming, not a scholarship to college. I have too much to do already."

"Not so much that she can't be on some stupid Dance Committee," Ivy muttered. I shushed Ivy, but I felt the same flare of irritation. It did sting a bit to have Miko choose them over us. How could you even compare a dumb dance to our magazine?

"Well, no, Meeky, *I'm* sorry," Shelby countered, in her dangerously silky be-very-careful tone. "But this has to take priority over everything. We have to win that School Spirit Award on Decade Day, and the only way to do that is to make sure everyone is working on their costumes. It's coming up at the end of this week—we've got to move on this. It's time for a major publicity blitz."

I didn't want to get caught eavesdropping, but I couldn't resist looking over to see how Miko was reacting to all this.

She was pressing her lips together tightly, looking like she was going to explode. I'd seen that look before—when we were trying to finish our first issue and had too much to do in too little time.

"Okay, so we'll need a design for an e-mail blast and some kind of logo to create a Facebook page. Plus, we need a list of everybody's numbers and e-mails," Shelby said.

Miko stood up so quickly her chair fell over. Without a word, she grabbed her bag and strode out of the library.

"Where's she going? She's not allowed to do that," Daphne complained. "We're supposed to stay here until the second period bell."

"Don't worry about it," barked Shelby.

Then she caught me looking at her. I looked away, but it was already too late.

"Incoming PQuit," murmured Ivy as Shelby stood up.

I sighed. A year ago I would have been flat-out scared to have called attention to myself from an angry PQuit. I'd come a long way in the last month, especially with Ivy's example. Ivy was somehow able to get along in school without getting too wrapped up in what people thought about her, said about her, or said to her face. She had a small smile on her face as Shelby flounced over to us.

"Paulie," Shelby said. "I've been looking everywhere for you."

What? There were so many things WRONG with that statement. Shelby had never called me Paulie in either of our lives. My locker was only three down from hers, and I had, in fact, been sitting within twelve feet of her for the last twenty minutes.

I decided not to point out any of these things and just gave Shelby a half smile.

She sat down, not even glancing at Tally and Ivy.

"So about this Homecoming feature we've been working on for *4 Girls*," Shelby said.

We?

"Uh, it's actually Ivy that's—"

"I've been thinking it would be a *lot* better if we focused the whole thing on one grade," Shelby said. "Say, the seventh grade. I mean, if the magazine is going to be the same length as the first issue, you don't really have that much room for lots of long articles. It would be much better to do a detailed piece on one grade than a vague one on the whole middle school."

"There's no way that—" Ivy began as Shelby stood up quickly.

"Great, Paulie. I'll text you later, and we can go into more detail," she called as she headed back toward her table.

Ivy and I watched, speechless, as Shelby took her place beside Daphne. They all leaned their heads together to whisper, presumably about Miko's unauthorized departure and their new Publicity Blitz—our magazine.

"Hello?" Ivy asked me. "Do I have laryngitis, too?"

"Apparently we both do," I said. "Either that, or our voices have morphed into some frequency Shelby's ears can't pick up. That was so obnoxious."

"What was she even talking about?" Ivy asked.

"I have no idea," I said. But apparently Tally did. She scribbled furiously, then shoved her pad toward me and Ivy.

Norah Alford posted on her Facebook page that the eighth-grade's Decade Day costumes are so awesome they are totally winning School Spirit Award this year. The winning grade gets an entire homework-free day, every subject! Shelby's all nuts about it now.

"Is that all?" I asked with a sigh. "There are so many bigger and more important things to be nuts about."

"Here comes Benny again," Ivy said.

What on earth was he doing? Benny was heading for my table, and he looked guilty or even a little nauseated, like he'd just eaten a whole cake by himself or something.

"Um, hey," Benny said. "Here's your, um . . . thing back. Thanks."

He handed me a folded-up piece of paper, then careened off behind one of the stacks.

"Is this the prank?" Ivy asked. "What is it?"

The PQuit table had fallen silent. Of course, they had noticed, too. The last thing I needed was for the PQuits to start gossiping about my Status with Benny. I didn't even know what my Status with Benny was! I didn't need anyone else giving me grief about it.

"It's just my social studies outline," I said loudly. "I must have left it on the . . ."

"Floor," Ivy suggested.

"Yeah, on the floor," I said.

I made a big deal out of putting it in my bag without looking at it. But the suspense was killing me. I hadn't lost any social studies notes. Was it a note? Benny had never given me a note. Why would he now? And why wouldn't the PQuits just stop watching me so I could look at the stupid thing?

Tally reached for her pad to make another comment and knocked over her travel mug. The top flew off, and tea splashed over the table and continued to glug out of the mug.

All three of us jumped up, grabbing our stuff off the table before the tea could reach it.

"What a spaz," I heard Daphne say with a snicker.

"I've got a bunch of tissues in my bag," Ivy said. "Hang on."

"Try to hurry. We're going to get detention if the librarian notices," I said. "You know how she is about drinks in the library."

Ivy produced a fistful of tissues and mopped up the mess while Tally watched, looking tearful.

"I'm sorry," she mouthed.

"It's no big deal," Ivy said. "No need to cry over spilled tea."

Tally scrawled something on her notebook and held it up.

I ruin everything—I am cursed!

"You're not cursed, Tal," I said.

"Just a little clumsy," Ivy added. She put an arm around Tally and gave her a friendly squeeze.

Nobody was looking at me at the moment. I grabbed Benny's note from my bag and opened it under the table. It was just two short lines.

I need to ask you something important. Can you find me at lunch?

I got a sudden flood of butterflies in my stomach. I was pretty sure this was not a Friend Question. I suddenly remembered Benny asking if I was going to Homecoming. He knew I hated school dances, but . . . *wow*.

Benny Novak was going to ask me to go to Homecoming with him.

BENNY NOVAK was going to ask *ME* to go to Homecoming with *HIM*.

I stuck the note back in my bag without saying anything. A year ago, I would have been ecstatic at the idea of Benny Novak asking me on a date. But this year, we had finally become friends. I really liked being friends with him. If it suddenly turned into a boy/girl thing, everything might be ruined. I didn't think I could stand that.

I caught Ivy looking at me. My little peek at the note had not escaped her. She knew me well enough to have an idea of what it had said from the expression on my face. She also knew me well enough to realize I didn't want to say anything about it.

"Hey, Tally," Ivy said. "What parts do you think Buster and Audriana will end up getting?"

Tally's face lit up, and she began writing something so complicated that she needed to add a diagram. Ivy and I watched her, as fascinated as if she were writing the secret location of the Holy Grail.

As I watched, I couldn't keep my mind from

wandering. Everything was changing—everyone was pretending something.

Ivy and I were both doing our best to pretend that everything was normal, that she was not moving away. I was pretending I was not about to become Benny's *un*friend. Tally was pretending that she still had a shot at the lead role in *Annie*. Miko was pretending *4 Girls*—and me, Ivy, and Tally, the rest of The Four—didn't matter. *ONE* thing needed to change.

Maybe Benny wants to tell me something else, I thought. *Maybe it's an idea for the magazine or a prank I can play on Kevin.*

By the time the bell for lunch rang later that day, I felt like I was spinning. There were so many thoughts in my head.

One step at a time, I thought.

There was no point in prolonging the agony. I went to the cafeteria and waited.

But Benny never showed up.

· chapter ·

13

I was standing in front of my gym locker in the girls' locker room, shoving my basketball sneakers and dirty socks into a plastic bag. Not only had Benny Novak failed to appear in the cafeteria yesterday, but he had failed to reappear at school today. I swung by the nurse's office to check the list, and sure enough, Benny Novak was out sick. He must have gotten the flu everyone else had. Part of me was relieved. The question of the dance could be avoided. At least for the next few days.

Audriana came racing into the locker room behind a group of other girls and made a beeline for me.

"Is she here? Have you talked to her?" she asked.

"Who?"

"Tally. She has gym next period. Where is she? The cast list is up! I want to make sure she knows."

"I haven't seen her, but you know Tally—she's

always running late. So? Who got Annie?"

The door opened and several more girls came in. None of them were Tally.

Audriana made a face.

"Valerie Stupid Teale," she said. "Big surprise. And she's strutting around like she's Lady Gaga or something. Soooo irritating."

"What about you?"

Audriana sighed. "I'm Daddy Warbucks's chauffeur. I get to sing a solo line in 'I Think I'm Gonna Like It Here,' but that's about it."

"What did Buster get?" I asked.

"Rooster," she replied. "It's not a huge part, but there are some really good scenes. He'll be fantastic."

I had to agree.

The door opened again. "Oh, there she is," I said.

"Y'all," Tally said, tossing her gym bag on the floor. "The world is *such* a cruel place."

Tally was back to normal, I noticed. Filled with Drama and *LOUD*.

"You saw the cast list?" Audriana asked. Tally nodded.

"Honestly, why do people not see how awful Valerie is?" Tally asked. "She's so fake and stilted—like she's trying to act like she thinks an actor playing Annie should act. Ugh. The whole thing is so completely unfair. The whole showcase is ruined now! Seriously,

I feel like somebody should do something about this. Bring Mr. Barrymore to his senses or lodge a complaint or something! I'm going to scream!"

Tally's voice had in fact been rising and was reaching the point of a screech that only dogs and bats could hear. It seemed like an overreaction. Even coming from Tally.

"Tal, I can't stand her, either," Audriana said. "But come on. The show isn't ruined. I didn't even get a decent part. I'm just some background character, and I don't feel like some injustice has been done or anything."

"But it's not the same for you," Tally said. "I mean, I know you get it—some of us are leading ladies and some of us aren't. Before I lost my voice, I really thought I had a shot at getting Annie."

Ouch.

"Tal, you might want to—" My voice was drowned out by the sound of the bell.

Audriana stood frozen, an odd look on her face that Tally didn't seem to notice.

"At least he's put up an understudy list," Tally said, rooting through her gym bag. "Now that my voice is back, there's no reason I can't sign up on that."

Audriana walked abruptly out of the locker room.

"Plus, Buster wants us to—" Tally looked around. "What happened to Audriana?"

"She took off," I said. "Listen, Tally, I don't know her all that well or anything, but . . . I don't know. Maybe Audriana is a little disappointed about her part, too."

Tally shook her head.

"Trust me, Audriana did not want to be Annie," Tally said. "I've been in enough shows with her to know that. It's Valerie Teale that's making her mad. She's such a diva!"

Tally pulled her gym shoes out of her bag, tossed the bag in the locker, and slammed it shut.

"Okay, well I'm going to run," I said.

Tally waved and began pulling her mass of curls into a tiny elastic band. I heard the elastic snap as I walked away and Tally squeal again.

$$\bullet \quad \bullet \quad \bullet \quad \bullet \quad \bullet \quad \bullet \quad \bullet$$

I got to bio just as the teacher, Mr. Pilsen, was arriving. I hated double-period science days. They combined our session with the AP class, where everyone was superbrilliant, and it felt like class went on forever.

There was an empty seat next to Miko. I hesitated for a moment. But when she looked up and saw me, she gave me a smile. I sat down, relieved that she was in a friendly mood. Maybe things didn't have to stay uncomfortable between us.

"How are you?" I asked. "How's your honors

project coming along? And everything else?"

"Okay," Miko said. "Everything is still really crazy. I think I'll finish my project by the deadline, but it's going to be close." Miko drew a few little sketches in her notebook. Then she turned to me, looking me straight in the eye. "Look, I know how it must seem to you guys. Me stepping back from 4 *Girls*, but then being on Shelby's Dance Committee."

"Oh," I said. "No. I mean, we did sort of wonder about it. But only a little."

Miko smiled. "Shelby is not good at taking no for an answer. I thought it would just be the one poster, but I was wrong. I've decided to quit the Homecoming Committee."

"Really?" I was shocked. Miko hadn't even completely quit 4 *Girls*.

Maybe there's still hope after all, I thought, trying not to get my hopes up.

"Yeah," Miko said, shrugging. "I meant it when I told you guys I just don't have any spare time. But I really want to do 4 *Girls* again. I don't even like doing dance posters."

"I kind of got that impression," I said. "Will Shelby be okay with it?"

Miko shrugged. "I don't know," she said. "She's my friend. She should be able to understand. But either way, I'm dropping out."

Our teacher, Mr. Pilsen, blew into the classroom like he'd been hurled by a catapult. "Okay, people, settle down and let's get started," he said. "Clear your desks of everything but two sharp pencils."

"What are we doing?" I asked Miko.

Miko was pulling two of the sharpest pencils I'd ever seen out of her pencil case.

"It's the unit test today, remember?" she asked.

I smacked my hand over my mouth.

"You forgot?" Miko whispered, her eyes wide.

I nodded, feeling my face turning a painful shade of red.

Not only had I forgotten the test was today, I had temporarily forgotten about bio altogether. I should have been going over the review sheets for the last two weeks. Being sick over the weekend wasn't going to excuse not studying. This was no simple quiz. A unit test would be 15 percent of my grade for the whole semester.

Mr. Pilsen was walking around passing out the tests. When I got mine, I quickly scanned the questions. I could tell immediately that I didn't know the answers to at least half of them. *AND* it wasn't a multiple choice test—guessing wouldn't work.

For the next forty-five minutes I sat clutching my pencil and trying not to look as paralyzed as I felt. Was there any feeling worse than completely blanking on a big test? Periodically, Miko would look over at me with a sympathetic expression. By the time Mr. Pilsen came around to collect the papers, I'd only managed to scribble a few sentences for each question.

"I tanked," I whispered to Miko on our way out of the room.

"Well, you were really sick this weekend," Miko offered. "Everyone knows how bad this flu is. Maybe you can talk to him. Ask to take a retest later."

I shook my head. Mr. Pilsen was extremely unforgiving when it came to missed work, and as far as he was concerned, I should have been diligently doing my review sheets long before I got the flu.

"Look, don't beat yourself up about it," Miko said. "You can't change it now. It's only one grade. Maybe you can do an extra credit project to get a few points added."

I nodded and smiled, not because I thought Miko's idea would help, but because she was being so nice to me. I still felt awful about the test, though.

I dragged myself through the remainder of the afternoon, trying to put the test out of my mind. Miko was right—I couldn't change it. I should focus on happier things, like the fact that Ivy was coming over to my house after school. We'd have some cookies, lie around and talk, compare notes on *4 Girls* . . . and I'd tell her about my test, and she would explain why it was okay. But even that thought made me feel bad, because before too long Ivy was going to be gone, too, and I was going to be alone again.

No. Focusing on happier things just wasn't going to do the trick.

• • • • • • •

I sat in my living room staring out the window at the street, looking for a car. I checked my phone to see if Ivy had texted that she was running late.

She hadn't. But I had an e-mail from Shelby Simpson.

▼ **To:** Paulina M. Barbosa
▼ **From:** SweetShelby
Subject: Homecoming Article

About the *4 Girls* Homecoming article—it will be much better if it only focuses on one grade, otherwise there will be way too much material. Miko agrees. Since The Four are all in seventh grade, and seventh grade is going to win Decade Day, obviously that's the one we should focus on. We will want to include a collage of photos of the best seventies outfits, and I will have Miko design it.

Unbelievable, I thought. *What must it be like going through life just assuming everyone is going to follow your orders?* And what did she mean about Miko agreeing? From what Miko had told me in bio, she was about to jump ship on Homecoming altogether.

I jumped at the sound of a knock on the door.

"Ivy!" I said happily as I threw the door open.

"So I got tons done on my article, and the cover is finished," Ivy said as she walked inside, talking like we were right in the middle of a conversation we'd been having for the last twenty minutes. "But we need that interview from Tally, and you and I have to decide how much space to set aside for Spirit Day pictures. *Please* tell me you have cookies."

I pointed to a plate on the living room table.

"Not just cookies," I said. "Girl Scout cookies."

"You have just made me very happy," Ivy said, heading for the plate. She took two Tagalongs, then looked up at me. "What? Should I put one back?"

I shook my head.

"What's wrong then?" Ivy asked.

"Nothing," I said, hanging my head a little. "You know—just . . . I'm going to miss this. And we barely even got to do anything."

Ivy chewed on her lower lip.

"I know," she said quietly. "I am so, so sorry."

"Why?" I cried. "It's not like it's your fault they're moving."

"No, definitely not," Ivy said. "I think the fact that they still refuse to just own it and tell me the truth is a good indicator of how important my feelings are. Ugh. Let's just . . . change the subject, okay?"

"Okay," I agreed quickly.

"Hand over that plate of Tagalongs," I said, and Ivy passed it to me. "So I've actually got a lot done, too. My 'Road to *Annie*' article is completely done up through today. I'll just need to add the review of the showcase, which I'm actually going to write after their dress rehearsal on tech week. That way we can get the issue out Monday morning when everyone's still talking about the play and Homecoming. Oh, speaking of which . . ."

I handed her my phone, the e-mail from Shelby still on-screen.

"You have got to be kidding me. Why does she think what she wants has any effect on *4 Girls*?" Ivy asked, shaking her head and handing back the phone.

"Because nobody ever says no to her," I replied. "Plus, she's best friends with Miko, so I guess she figures she's practically one of us."

"Oh, please," Ivy said, dropping her bag on the living room floor and flopping over on the couch. "Miko isn't even one of *us* anymore. And the fact that she's miraculously found the time to work on that Dance Committee stuff is really bugging me. I think we should just make it official and let her quit."

"No," I said quickly. "Let's just give it a little longer. Please?" I couldn't say anything about Miko's plans to dump the Dance Committee. After all, what if she changed her mind? But I believed she was going to do it and that she'd be back with The Four one hundred percent by the time the second issue was done. Of course, we still wouldn't be The Four, because now Ivy was moving away. Whatever happened, we weren't going to be *four* ever again.

"Okay, so business is taken care of," Ivy said. "Now let's get down to the really important issue."

"Which is?" I prompted.

"Benny Novak," Ivy said. "He's not going to be out sick forever. You need to figure out what you're going to do when he gets back."

"Why?" I asked weakly.

"You know perfectly well *why*," Ivy said. She grabbed another Tagalong and took a bite out of it. "You know as well as I do that he's going to ask you to that dance. It is my job, my duty, as your best friend, to talk you out of this ridiculous idea that going out with him is a bad thing."

I groaned.

"I don't want to talk about this," I said. "It makes me all nervous."

"Tough," Ivy said. "Now let's start at the beginning. You first realized you liked him last year, and . . ."

"And so Evelyn tried to help, and it backfired. You heard that whole story."

"Yup. So then what? When did it feel like things

really started to change?"

"This year, definitely. During the whole competition, he kept asking about *4 Girls*, how it was going. Then he sent that copy to his uncle, which helped get the extra money . . . somewhere in there, things got easier."

"Okay, so it's easier now. What's the problem?"

I got comfortable next to Ivy as I tried to explain how going on a date with your friend might ultimately leave you friendless *and* boyfriendless, and how could that be worth it.

And, knowing Ivy, she wasn't going to get off that couch until one of two things happened—I accepted her suggestion that going out with Benny would be fun or we ran out of Girl Scout cookies.

· chapter ·

14

The next day, when I'd forgotten all about tanking in bio, I was given a friendly reminder. Mr. Pilsen always returned tests on Wednesdays, and here was mine placed like a gift in front of me. It had a huge red F on the front. Some gift.

"Okay, well, at least it's officially over with," Miko said, looking over my shoulder at the test. "You failed. It's done. Now you can move past it."

"Except Mr. Pilsen makes you get a parent's signature on a failed test," I said. "To prove you told them about it."

Miko made a face. "He's so mean," she said. "Are you going to get in trouble?"

"My mother won't exactly be thrilled," I said. "But she'll be okay about it. She's more likely to obsess on what Subconscious Adolescent Issue caused me to flunk a test. I usually do pretty well in school, and she's not the type to put the pressure on or anything."

"You're lucky," Miko said as we walked toward our lockers.

I knew Miko's parents were the exact opposite. They put a huge amount of pressure on her. When we were working on the first issue of *4 Girls*, I felt like I'd gotten a few glimpses of the real Miko—the one that existed beneath the pressure from her parents and from the PQuits. And I had liked what I'd seen.

"So how's the new issue coming?" Miko asked.

"Oh, it's great," I said. "I mean, it's not the same without you because we're doing the design ourselves, and we don't exactly have your gift for it. I think we can just get away with it this time. I'm really excited about our features. I think people are going to have a lot of fun with it."

"I can't wait to see it," Miko said. "I really mean that. I'm hating having to sit this one out."

Sit this one out, I thought, suppressing a smile. *She didn't say quit. She's going to come back.*

We'd reached our lockers. Shelby Simpson was standing in front of hers, examining her reflection in a mirror she had hung inside the door. I knew I shouldn't look too chatty with Miko now that Shelby was standing there. I'd accepted that Miko had to tone things down with me when her best friend was around. Shelby was Head PQuit, and she didn't like me. And when Shelby didn't like someone, none of the PQuits were supposed to like them, either. You had to pick your battles in the seventh grade. This was one I wasn't going to fight.

Shelby caught sight of us in the mirror and turned around.

"Paulina, I got this ridiculous e-mail from that Ivy girl about our Homecoming article. You and I really need to talk about this *4 Girls* thing," Shelby said. "Also, Meeky, you have got to get that e-mail blast out tonight about Decade Day—it's practically here. Even if you're up till midnight, just make sure that e-mail blast gets out to everybody. And about the article, you've just got to understand that it needs to—"

"Shelby, I'm sorry," I interrupted. "But like I'm sure Ivy told you in her e-mail, it's her article, not mine. And she's covering all the grades participating in the Homecoming events. And I happen to agree with her. *4 Girls* is for everyone."

Shelby narrowed her eyes.

"What is your problem?" she snapped.

"I don't have a problem," I replied coolly.

Actually, I had many problems. This just didn't happen to be one of them.

"Maybe you need to rethink this," Shelby said, putting her hands on her hips. "Right, Miko?"

"Wrong, Shelby." My mouth dropped open at Miko's words.

"I'm with Paulina," Miko continued. "It's Ivy's call, and it would be lame of *4 Girls* to only feature their own grade. And if you want an e-mail blast so badly, put it together yourself."

O. M. G. Miko was really doing it. She was standing up to Shelby Simpson. In front of me. A non-PQuit.

"What's lame is when other people refuse to do what they're *supposed* to," Shelby shot back, glaring at Miko.

"So now you're in charge of what I'm supposed to be doing?" Miko snapped.

Shelby glowered, then turned and slammed her locker shut.

"I'm the head of the seventh-grade Dance Committee. You are on the committee. So yeah. I'm in charge of what you're supposed to be doing," Shelby stated.

"Well, that's easy to fix," Miko said. "I quit."

Shelby's eyes grew wide, and her face turned a deep red.

"Don't be crazy," Shelby said. "You can't quit."

"Well, I just did," Miko said. "I don't have time for this, Shel. I don't have time for anything until my honors project is handed in. I keep telling you that, and you don't listen. But you know what? If I don't

135

have time to work on *4 Girls*, then I'm not working on your thing, either."

"*My* thing?" Shelby exclaimed. "It's our thing!"

"But it isn't," Miko said. "Or maybe it was once, and it just isn't anymore. But I'm out, Shelby."

Shelby glared at Miko for a few moments. Then she narrowed her eyes. "You know what? You are out, Miko. You are all the way out."

With that declaration, Shelby spun on her heel and marched off down the hall.

Miko sighed.

"I'm sorry," I said. "I feel like that was partly my fault."

Miko looked surprised. "Not at all. I told her when she asked that I didn't have much time, and she just acts like she doesn't hear me. So I'm out. It's done."

The bell for the beginning of lunch rang.

"Are you going to the cafeteria?" I asked. "We're supposed to have one of our *4 Girls* mini-meetings. I mean, you're welcome to come if you want."

Miko hesitated, looking down the hall in the direction Shelby had stalked off.

"I'm not really hungry," she said. "I'm just going to go to the library and get a jump on my homework."

I nodded. It was one thing to face Shelby down in the hallway when it was just us. It was quite another to deal with a lunch table of PQuits when half the middle school was sitting within earshot.

"Catch you later then," I said.

So now Shelby and Miko are on the outs, I thought as I got my lunch out of my locker. They'd been best friends since fourth grade. I'd seen plenty of PQuits come and go, but Miko and Shelby had always been tight. I thought of Evelyn and Ivy moving away. I got a bad feeling in my stomach. I was happy that Miko had stood up for herself, but nobody should have to lose their best friend.

I ran into Ivy paying for a couple of milks at the cashier.

"Hey," she said. "I'm sitting in back with Tally. Her supporting cast is with her. I don't think she's going to be too focused on the meeting. She's experiencing acute Teale-itis."

Ivy had been calling all of Tally's *Annie*-related mood swings Teale-itis for the last week.

"Poor Tally," I said. "It's bad enough that Valerie got the part, but from what I hear, she's being even more obnoxious than she was when the cast list went up."

"Yep. That's bad karma for Valerie. Sooner or later it will come back to get her. Listen, I finished my 'Slice of Life' survey for the magazine. The pie chart looks great—I'm going to e-mail it to you tonight."

"That's fabulous," I said. "The articles are done

137

now, so all we'll need are the photos of Decade Day, a wrap-up of Homecoming Week after the fact, and the review of *Annie*, and we're good to go! And with more than a week to spare!"

"Don't forget the Mr. Barrymore interview," Ivy reminded me. "Tally did e-mail him the questions, so I'm sure we'll have it soon."

"We will," I said. "So listen, Miko just quit the Dance Committee!"

"What?"

I nodded. "I was standing right there. She told Shelby she didn't have the time and that she didn't agree with her trying to pressure you to focus your piece on our grade. Then she quit. Shelby was really mad."

"Huh," Ivy said thoughtfully. "She *really* quit?"

I nodded. "She told me in bio that she liked working on *4 Girls* better. She's going to come back, Ivy."

"Boy," Ivy said. "That's the last thing I expected. Well, good for Miko! That took guts."

"I know, right?" I agreed. "I thought she would—"

The rest of my sentence was drowned out by the sound of someone launching loudly and aggressively into song.

"They'll be there calling me baaaaaby . . . maaaaaaybe!"

Valerie Teale was standing at a table by the window,

delivering her swan song to an enraptured audience. They burst into applause, hooting and cheering as she finished. Valerie took a deep bow, then turned toward the table where Buster and Audriana were sitting with Tally and blew her a not-so-gracious kiss.

"Ignore her," Ivy said to Tally as we reached the lunch table. "She's a show-off."

"She's an idiot," Buster added.

"She's *Annie*," Tally moaned, putting her hands over her face.

"Maybe she's just doing that method acting thing," Audriana said. "Living the part and all that."

"She's gloating," Tally shot back. "It's completely inappropriate. That is not how a leading lady is supposed to act!"

"Well, I wouldn't know about that," Audriana muttered. "You know, since I'm not a leading lady myself."

"And she's got two and a half weeks left to lord it over everyone," Buster said, shaking his head. "What a diva."

"Mr. Barrymore ought to do something about it," Tally said. "It's not fair."

"Maybe he doesn't realize how she's treating people," Audriana suggested. "Maybe she doesn't even realize it. Maybe a person can be rude and insensitive and have no clue that's what they're doing."

Uh. Oh. I didn't think I could handle watching another best-friend-duo break up this week. *Come on, Tal*, I thought.

But Tally rolled her eyes, completely missing Audriana's point.

"She knows exactly what she's doing," Tally said. "And I'm sure Mr. Barrymore notices when one of his actors is trying to create a peeking order."

"I think it's called a pecking order," Ivy suggested.

"Exactly!" Tally said. "I mean, no offense, Audriana, but you kind of have to have been there to understand what it's like to be cast in a starring role."

From the look on Audriana's face, I suspected that Tally's "no offense" had not worked.

"Just make sure Valerie doesn't find out about the secret agent," Buster warned. "She'd probably toss you under a bus to get to him first. Have you found a picture of him yet?"

"I have some very good clues I'm tracking down," Tally said mysteriously. "But it's getting complicated. I'm not finding Mr. Barrymore's agent's information on the New York websites that are supposed to list everybody. But I will find him, and I'll figure out what he looks like, and when he shows up on opening night, I'm going to be right there to meet him. And I'm going to knock his socks off."

"Spoken like a true leading lady," Ivy said, grinning.

I snuck a glance at Audriana. She was rolling her eyes and stabbing at her spaghetti with a plastic fork.

At that moment, though I can't possibly explain it, something made me turn around and look toward the cafeteria door.

Benny Novak was standing in the doorway. He seemed to catch sight of me at the same moment I did him.

He sort of gestured toward the hallway with his head. Just a quick nod, then he turned and walked out.

"Paulie, go on," Ivy said softly. "We talked about this. You can't avoid him forever, and at some point he's going to give up. And if that happens, I for one will repeatedly be saying 'I told you so.'"

"But what if I . . . what if . . ."

"Give me a break," Ivy told me, nudging my arm. "So your friendship might change if he asks you on a date. At this point, your friendship has already changed. Just go for it! Do not make me give the whole 'What if the Wright brothers had been afraid of crashing?' speech. Because do you know what would have happened? Someone else would have invented the airplane. And the Wright brothers would have spent the rest of their lives wishing they'd taken a gamble on something."

She was right. I knew that.

"What's going on? What are we talking about?" Buster asked.

"Do I . . ."

"You look fine," Ivy said. "Wait, just . . ." She reached up and unclipped the comb holding my hair up. Then she tucked one strand behind my ear and straightened both my earrings.

"Perfect," she said.

"Will somebody please translate?" Buster said. "I can't stand not knowing what's going on."

"Okay," I said. "Okay. I'm going."

"Going where?" Buster demanded, sounding almost beside himself with frustration.

I had so many butterflies in my stomach I felt like I might spontaneously levitate.

"To talk to Benny Novak, I'm guessing," Audriana said.

"Paulina and Benny are soul mates," Tally said matter-of-factly. "They come from the same star stuff. They've probably reincarnated together tons of times. They—"

"Tal, please," I snapped. "That's not helping right now." I stood up so quickly I felt a little dizzy.

"And, Paulie," Ivy added. "Don't forget to breathe."

I took a deep breath and walked as fast as I could without looking like I was in a rush. When I stepped out of the cafeteria, I looked around. Benny was standing a little ways down the hallway, leaning against a wall. Waiting for *ME*. I walked toward him, trying to imagine how a person ought to walk to give the impression that nothing particularly out of the ordinary was going on.

"Hey," I said.

"Hey," Benny answered.

"Are you feeling better? I mean, after the flu?" I added.

"Yeah, I am. I mean, it took a while. That was a nasty bug."

"I know," I told him. "At least we don't have to worry about catching it now. We're, like, safe for the year. We have Diplomatic Flu Immunity."

Benny laughed, and I relaxed a little bit.

"So listen, I know the next bell is about to ring and all that, so . . . the Homecoming Dance is three days away, and I know it's not really your thing, but I figured you'd go since you're putting it in your next issue and all that."

"Oh. I mean, yeah, I am," I said.

"Okay. So do you want to go with me then?"

Wow. That was it? He had asked me on a date, just like that. No big deal, no earthquake. I was not dead. I had not accidentally made a high-pitched squealing noise. This wasn't awkward at all. In fact . . . it was kind of nice.

"Sure," I said with a smile.

"Cool," Benny told me. "Then it's a date."

One small step for mankind. One giant step for ME!

Except, what did you talk about right after the perfect guy asked you out on a date?

The bell rang. Perfect timing.

"See you later," he said.

"Later," I replied as casually as I could.

I turned and walked away just like I did every ordinary, boring day in school. But this time, I knew there was something extremely different about me. I was a girl with a date. With a guy I was already friends with. And really liked.

I only had a few minutes to get to class, but I doubled back toward the cafeteria, where people were streaming out. I almost collided with Ivy.

"Well?" she said when she saw me.

I grabbed her arm and opened my mouth in an enormous, silent Scream of Joy. Ivy grabbed my arm back and squeezed.

"Told you!" Ivy exclaimed. "I've got a dentist appointment after school, but I want to hear every single thing. I'll call you tonight, okay?"

"You better!"

And I added another silent Scream of Joy, just because I felt like it. Then I hightailed it to class.

• • • • • • •

"It was just so easy," I said, repeating more or less the same thing for about the sixth time. "It was like he was asking me if I liked dogs or if I'd done my social studies homework."

"Because you're already friends," Ivy said. "The hard part was done."

My ear was getting tired from having the phone pressed against it, so I switched the receiver to the other side.

"I was just so sure it would be awkward and embarrassing," I said.

"You don't say," Ivy remarked. "And once again, I told you so. Didn't I?"

"You did," I confirmed. "You are a fantastic, wise friend."

"Don't forget stylish," Ivy said.

"And stylish," I added. "A fantastic, wise, stylish friend. I do not know *what* I'd do without you."

There was a pause. I didn't want to remember Ivy was moving.

"Anyway . . . ," Ivy said.

"Yeah, anyway," I echoed.

A chirp came from my laptop.

"Huh, I've got an e-mail," I said.

"Me too," Ivy said. "Uh-oh. Mine's from the Dowager Empress Shelby."

I tapped on the **1** in my in-box.

"So's mine. Look at the recipient list—it's to the whole class," I pointed out.

I opened the e-mail. It was an extremely colorful, not-too-adeptly Photoshopped collage of seventies stuff from *Charlie's Angels* to a cartoon of Elton John in platform shoes and massive pink sunglasses with lenses the shape of stars. In huge, bold caps in the center was text that read:

▼ **To:** Everyone
▼ **From:** SweetShelby
Subject: Decade Day!

A FINAL REMINDER FROM THE DANCE COMMITTEE—TOMORROW ALL SEVENTH-GRADERS WILL COME TO SCHOOL DRESSED IN AN OUTFIT FROM OUR HOMECOMING DECADE, THE 1970S. WE ARE IN THIS TO WIN—PUT YOUR HEART INTO IT! BEST DRESSED WILL BE FEATURED IN THIS MONTH'S ISSUE OF *4 GIRLS* MAGAZINE!

"The girl never gives up, does she?" I said. "And what's this about the best dressed being 'featured' in the magazine? She can't say that—all we ever said was that we'd be putting some pictures in. Anyway, I'm totally not dressing up in some seventies outfit. I mean, you're not, are you, Ivy?"

"Nothing in the universe could get me into polyester hip-huggers and platform shoes," Ivy said. "But even if I was willing to make an exception for Decade Day, I wouldn't dress up *tomorrow*."

"Why not?" I asked.

"Because, Einstein, tomorrow is Thursday. Decade Day is Friday. Shelby got herself in such a state over this, she got her dates mixed up."

I looked at the e-mail again. Shelby's e-mail was ordering everyone to dress up *tomorrow*. One day too early.

"You are totally right—she got the date wrong! Do you think people are going to show up in their outfits on the wrong day?"

Ivy laughed.

"I don't know," she said. "But you know what I do know? I'm going to be sure to bring my camera to school tomorrow."

· chapter ·
15

Ivy might have noticed the Decade Day date error, but apparently not everybody did. I was at my locker before first period when Shelby, Daphne, and Charelle came down the hall in full seventies outfits.

Daphne was wearing a pair of plaid polyester pants with a superhigh waist. She had matched it with a yellow peasant blouse and a huge, gold pendant that declared DISCO RULES. Her purse was a bright-green nylon bag that said LE SPORTSAC all over it, and on her head, she wore a baseball cap covered in silver sequins. Charelle was sporting a lime-green skort with white kneesocks and chunky denim-covered shoes. A pair of enormous, white plastic sunglasses with cherry-red lenses covered half her face. But neither of them had anything on Shelby Simpson. The Head of the PQuits would never be outdone.

Shelby was wearing a pair of cream-colored satin

pants that flared into massive bell-bottoms, which were covered in spatterings of blue sequins. She had a shiny jacket of electric blue that was covered with words like BOOGIE NIGHTS, GET FUNKY, and DISCO DIVA. Her hair had been fashioned into a bizarre style, with all the parts in front curled so they flew back from her head in rolled wings. Perhaps the most amazing thing was her shoes—blue vinyl platform shoes with a heel that must have been five inches high. It was a miracle she could even stand in them.

The three of them stood together, posing by the lockers. They looked extremely pleased with themselves. When a group of sixth-graders in their regular clothes stopped to stare at them, Shelby nudged Daphne.

"Losers don't even have outfits," she said. "Nice school spirit, midgets."

More students arrived, gawking at the PQuits and pointing at them. All of them were dressed in their normal school clothes.

A PQuit-in-Training dashed up to Shelby—she was wearing a shiny, gold jumpsuit and something that looked like a sombrero covered in fake fur.

"Shel, is this good? Is this okay? You look soooo much better than me!"

Shelby ignored her. Her smug expression had begun to fade as she looked around. The more kids who showed up in their regular clothes, the more confused she looked.

A tall, skinny girl with jet-black hair stepped forward and stood with her hands on her hips, checking out the PQuits from head to toe.

"I've got to say, you seventh-graders really know how to get attention," the girl said.

"We've got school spirit, which is more than I can say for you, Norah," Shelby shot back.

"Oh, I've got plenty of school spirit, and I plan to flaunt it. On Decade Day. Which is tomorrow!"

Shelby looked absolutely flabbergasted. Her face flushed crimson. It was pretty funny, but at the same time, I felt bad for Shelby. I have this recurring dream where I show up at school in my pajamas. When I wake up and realize it's only a nightmare, I always feel relieved.

But Shelby Simpson's Fashion Nightmare was really happening.

Shelby looked frozen in place. It was the first time she'd ever seemed to have no idea what to do. Daphne and Charelle stood on either side of her like disco bodyguards. But they looked just as shocked.

Someone else pushed through the crowd toward Shelby. It was Miko. My eyes grew wide with surprise.

Miko was wearing a rayon, white pantsuit and vest, under which she sported a red satin shirt with an enormous, pointy collar. Her patent leather, red shoes matched the shirt perfectly. She had several fat, gold chains around her neck and a big, round button pinned to her jacket that read I'VE GOT SATURDAY NIGHT FEVER in sparkly lettering.

"Girls, you look fabulous!" Miko said loudly.

Norah was laughing so hard she was practically bent over. Shelby was trying to move behind Charelle and Daphne in an attempt to hide.

But it was way too late for that.

"Hey look, everybody, I just happen to have my camera with me!" Norah announced.

Miko stepped up next to her friends and turned toward Norah. "Definitely! Take our picture!" she said enthusiastically.

Shelby was still trying to hide, but Miko pulled her forward and put one arm around her. She wrapped her other arm around Daphne. Charelle and the PQuit-in-Training, accustomed to following the others' lead, stepped up and linked arms, too.

"Okay, ready? And one, two, three, say 'Seventies Cheese'!" Miko said cheerfully, smiling at the camera.

Norah took the picture, the flash making Daphne's silver-sequined hat light up like a supernova.

"Awesome," Miko declared as the first bell rang. "Now we all better do the hustle, people, or we're going to be late for class!"

Everyone started moving off down the hallway toward their classrooms. Shelby stood there looking dazed, Miko's arm still around her.

"See you guys at lunch?" Miko asked. "We can have, like, a seventies-only table. You have to be in costume or you can't sit there."

Shelby looked at Miko and her face brightened. "Yeah, that would be cool. Seventies-only table!" Shelby said. She hoisted her book bag over her shoulder and teetered down the hall on her dangerously high platform shoes, Charelle and Daphne trailing behind her.

"Nice outfit," I said to Miko. She actually did look kind of chic.

"Thanks," Miko replied with a grin. "I figured you couldn't get much more seventies than the John Travolta disco suit."

We both had class on the second floor, so we walked toward the stairs together.

"But listen—Shelby's e-mail blast had the wrong date," I told Miko apologetically. "Decade Day isn't today—it's tomorrow."

"I know," Miko said. "But I didn't open my e-mail until after eleven last night. By the time I noticed the mistake, it was too late to call everyone."

"Wait. You knew today wasn't Decade Day? And you wore your disco suit, anyway?"

Miko shrugged and nodded.

"Why?"

"Shelby's my friend," Miko said. "I figured if she was going to look silly, I might as well look silly, too. Strength in numbers and all that."

This wasn't the first time I thought I'd figured Miko out only to have her surprise me.

"That was really cool of you," I said.

"Well, you know," she said. "What are friends for?"

So Miko hadn't lost her best friend after all. I was truly glad for her. There was nothing in the world like a best friend. In her own way, Miko had stepped up to be a leading lady, too.

· **chapter** ·
16

The next day the PQuits dutifully returned in their seventies outfits for the actual Decade Day, and this time they had plenty of company. I'm still not into the whole Homecoming/school spirit thing, but I have to admit the Decade Day thing was a small stroke of genius. Not that I'd ever tell Shelby I thought so. Fridays were always better than other school days, but this one in particular was an awesome time. The fact that the winner of the School Spirit Award ended up being the eighth-graders might have ruined it for Shelby, but not for me.

Ivy took me to the mall after school because she'd seen the perfect dress for me to wear to the Homecoming Dance.

"Am I right, or am I right?" Ivy asked, standing next to me as I stared at my reflection in the mirror of the dressing room. The dress was made of soft, sweaterlike material. It was a deep burgundy-red, and it fit me perfectly. Ivy had picked out a pair of textured red-and-gold tights to go with it.

"Plus, I have a pair of gorgeous, knee-high suede boots in chocolate-brown you can borrow. They'll go perfectly," she told me, fussing a little with my hair.

"How do you do that?" I asked. "This dress looks like it was made for me."

Ivy gave me a wide smile of satisfaction.

"I know clothes, that's all," she said. "It's one of my many gifts."

My own smile faded a little. It seemed like there wasn't any moment I could enjoy with Ivy that wasn't now tinged with the upsetting knowledge that she'd be leaving.

"Come on," Ivy said, seeing my face change. "Let's get this paid for so we can go get a smoothie. Or fries maybe. I might be in the mood for fries."

We ended up in the food court with smoothies AND fries and a text from Tally saying she was on her way over because she needed to talk.

"You don't mind that I told her okay, do you, Ivy? It sounded like she might have something on her mind."

"Oh, that's unusual indeed!" Ivy said, with a little wink, digging at her smoothie with the straw.

"So . . . still no details on the . . . thing?" I asked. I

didn't want to know, but I hated not knowing, too.

"No," Ivy said. "And it's getting ridiculous. My mom goes into her home office and has these major conference calls negotiating all the details of her new job—I mean it's on speakerphone! Hello, I have ears! And still, nobody has said a word to me!"

"Well, have you asked?" I probed gently.

Ivy picked up a french fry and broke it in half.

"No," she said quietly. "And obviously I should. I should just confront them—this is my life we're talking about."

"So . . . why don't you?"

Ivy sighed.

"I guess I'm sort of feeling stubborn now, like I want to see how long they're going to just arrange my life around me without including me in the conversation."

"Well, you can't do that," I said firmly. "It's gone on long enough. You have to talk to them about this, Ivy. Promise me. Promise that sometime between now and Monday you'll ask them to level with you."

Ivy took a long sip of smoothie, her eyes on mine.

"I hate it when you get all wise and sensible," she said. "Okay, yeah. I promise."

"Good," I said, relieved and not relieved at the same time. "Oh, there's Tally."

Tally was making her way through the tables at the

food court. She didn't look like her usual, bubbly self.

"Hey, y'all," she said, sitting in an empty seat next to Ivy. "Okay, so I have big news for you."

"Let me guess—Valerie asked you to take over Annie for her," I said.

"Nope," Tally said, rummaging through her bag. "I said big news, not great news. No—I found this at the library."

Tally plunked a huge, dog-eared paperback onto the table. The title was *Professional Theater Marketplace National Directory*.

"What's that?" Ivy asked.

"It lists every actor in the country who's registered with Actors' Equity. It also lists all agents and theaters. Remember how I was trying to find Gideon Barrymore's agent?"

"Yeah," I said. "Still can't find his?"

"Oh, it's here," Tally said. "So is Mr. Barrymore. And so is the big, fat, ugly truth."

"What are you talking about, Tal?" I asked.

Tally was flipping through the book furiously. She stopped at one page and pointed at it.

"This. This is what I'm talking about!"

Ivy pulled the book toward her, looked at the page, then looked back up, her expression confused.

"What am I looking at, Tal?" she asked.

Tally tapped the page with one finger.

"It's all right there. Gideon Barrymore is a liar. Gideon Barrymore is a fake!"

Ivy and I exchanged a quick glance.

"What are you talking about?" I asked. "We see him every day. You found his IMDb page. We saw him on *Nebula Wars*!"

Tally shook her head.

"No, I'm talking about all of his 'I'm a professional' stuff—his Broadway this and Manhattan that."

"Are you saying he made something up?"

Tally shook her head

"No. I mean, yes. He's from Manhattan all right. It says so right here in his listing. Manhattan, *Kansas*! And yeah, he's done a couple of Broadway shows. At the Elm Street Broadway House! He's a fraud!"

My mouth dropped open. Ivy looked like she might laugh, but she stopped herself.

"There's a Manhattan, Kansas?" she asked.

Tally's face was red with anger.

"Gideon Barrymore isn't even his real name—it's *Barry Moore*. Not Gideon. Just plain old Barry."

"Okay, I think we can all cut someone slack for not wanting to be called Barry," Ivy said with a small smile.

"It's not funny!" Tally exclaimed, looking tearful. "Guys, I don't know what to do. I feel like he pulled something over on us—like he's been lying

158

to everyone. Am I supposed to tell on him? Am I supposed to pretend like I don't know and just show up to rehearsal tomorrow and look grateful while he gives everybody his big, important actor guy directions?"

"Okay, slow down a sec," I said, fumbling with my phone. "Let me pull up his website again."

I found the entry on Barrymore and read it.

"Okay, Tal, it doesn't actually say anything that isn't true here," I said. "It says he lives and works in Manhattan. It doesn't say anything about New York. And it says something about Broadway credits, but it doesn't specify . . . um, which Broadway he's talking about. So you can't really say he's a fraud."

"He's making himself look like something he's not," Tally said. "Isn't that dishonest?"

"Okay, wait," Ivy said. "First of all, Paulie, she does have a point. I lived in New York City all my life until we moved here. When someone says Manhattan, people are going to assume they mean New York. And when an actor refers to Broadway, people are also going to take that as New York. I mean, if someone told you that they were an astronaut, it would be logical to think they meant that they took rockets into space, right? So if it turned out that astronaut was actually just the name of their bowling league . . . that is kind of lying. Or at the very least, it's making yourself out to be someone you aren't by using false pretenses."

"That's what I thought," Tally said. "I sent him the interview by e-mail like you said, and the whole thing is done. But now I know this! How can we put the interview in the magazine now?"

"But at the same time—" Ivy continued, holding one hand up to quiet Tally, "you said those are listings of members of Actors' Equity, right?"

Tally nodded, frowning.

"Okay, well Actors' Equity is a professional organization. My sister Nat dated this guy a few years back who did a summer internship at Equity. I'm no expert, but I do know that you can't just sign up to be a member. You have to have some kind of professional credits—you have to qualify. So you can't really say the guy is *pretending* to be a professional actor."

"But . . . you said . . . you . . ." Tally looked desperately confused.

"Okay," I said. "Let's just think this through. You're right that Mr. Barrymore has kind of created some misleading ideas about himself. That's definitely not good. But with all the time I've spent watching you guys get this production together, from everything I've heard people say, the guy is a decent director. Everyone seems to like him, and it looks to me like he's been doing a great job. Am I wrong about that?"

"I *thought* he was," Tally said grudgingly. Then she tapped the book again. "But this changes all that."

"No, it doesn't," Ivy said gently. "Either he's a good director or he isn't. I don't think you can attach conditions to that. His story isn't what you wanted it to be, or I guess what he wanted it to be. So he's a regular guy who messes up just like anyone else. But how has he treated you, Tal—how has he treated everybody he's working with here?"

Tally took a deep breath and looked at the floor for a moment.

"He is always respectful, and he is always professional," she said firmly.

"Okay," I said. "So I think we should do the same. The interview is about *Annie* and about why he became an actor, right?"

Tally nodded.

"So it's fine then," I told her.

"So we should just keep that interview with him in *4 Girls*, just like nothing ever happened?" she asked.

"Nothing *did* happen," I pointed out quietly. "Except that he let you down a little."

"But then . . . do I tell people? Do I keep it a secret?"

"That's up to you, Tally," I said. "I guess you just have to ask yourself if it would affect Mr. Barrymore, if it would affect the actors actually, if you spread this around. Are people going to lose confidence in him? And if they do, will they lose confidence in the showcase, too?"

Tally stared at the book in front of her for several moments. Then she closed it.

"You're right," she said. "Mr. Barrymore is still a good director and it's still a great show and that's all that matters. I'm not going to breathe a word about this."

Ivy clapped her hands.

"Good for you, Tally," she said. "And for the record, you're showing some pretty amazing investigative reporter skills there."

"Am I?" Tally said, her eyes shining.

"Oh yeah," Ivy said. Her phone, which was on the table in front of her, buzzed.

"Don't answer that!" Tally said quickly.

Ivy shot me an amused look.

"It's a text message," she told Tally. "But just out of curiosity, why didn't you want me to answer my own cell phone?"

"Because there are three planets coming into alignment this week, and if you happen to be talking on a cell phone at the precise moment the alignment begins, you can jump out of phased time."

Ivy was holding back a smile. "Which means . . . ," she urged.

"Which means you'd start falling behind everybody

else, by just a couple of seconds every hour, but it adds up. After a week, it would be three for you, but four o'clock for everybody else! Eventually you get trapped in your own past! Seriously, y'all, it's true! I saw it on the news!"

"I am deeply grateful that you've alerted us to this," Ivy said.

Tally nodded, her eyes growing very round and clear.

"I know, right?" she murmured. "I was stuck in the past once before, and believe me, y'all, it is no fun!"

It's so nice to know that some things stay the same. No matter what else went on in the world, life with Tally Janeway meant there was never a dull moment.

· chapter ·
17

We managed to make it halfway through the next week with no drama whatsoever. But all that changed on Wednesday, when Ivy and I were sitting on a bench outside the cafeteria eating our sandwiches and enjoying an unusually warm October day.

Tally rushed over. She was wearing a long, crushed purple dress that made her look like a cross between a Hogwarts professor and a sixties rock star. Her hair was all over the place—she looked like she'd been outside playing in a windstorm.

"Here you both are," Tally exclaimed, lunging toward us.

She looked like a charging lion that had overvolumized its mane.

"Y'all cannot believe it. You can't!"

I knew better than to guess what it was I would not believe. It could be anything from a tweet about a spaceship landing to a sighting of the cast of the *Twilight* movies at the local zoo.

"What's going on?" I asked.

Tally perched on the edge of the bench, so breathless she could get only a few words out at a time.

"Valerie Tee . . . ," she breathed.

"Teale . . . ," Ivy prompted.

Tally nodded as she gulped more air. "Just went home with the fuuu . . ."

I stared at Tally. "With the flu?"

Tally shrieked and grabbed my arms, nodding wildly.

"Yes! Valerie Teale has the flu!"

"Didn't I say that girl's bad karma would come back to her?" Ivy asked. She took another bite of her sandwich.

"But what does this mean?" I asked. "What do you do about the showcase?"

"Mr. Barrymore posted a notice on the bulletin board outside the office. There's an emergency meeting called for three in the auditorium today," Tally said, jumbling one word over the next. "No one knows for sure what will happen. But there's only a week and a half until our first dress rehearsal, that's the one you're seeing so you can do the review, Paulie. Mr. Barrymore might feel like it's too risky to see how long she takes to get better."

"In which case . . ."

"They'd have to pick someone to step into the part! An understudy!"

"Tally, wow," I said.

"Right?" she cried. "Because he had a sign-up sheet out a few weeks ago for people who wanted to understudy, and I signed up!"

"Wow, wow, wow . . . ," I said. "I mean . . . wow. So—"

"So you guys have to come with me to the emergency meeting today!" Tally said. "It could be a huge moment for the *4 Girls* article. An enormous, unforeseen tragedy that is the unwitting birth of a new, young Broadway star!"

"But Mr. Barrymore had that sign up about only actors being allowed in," Ivy reminded Tally.

She shook her head.

"No, that was just for the audition week," she assured me. "And it's not like you're just some random people. You're with *4 Girls*! We did an interview with him—we're featuring the play!"

"Look, I'll try, okay?" I promised her. "If we're allowed in, I'll definitely go."

"Me too," Ivy said.

Tally's eyes were shining.

"Oh, thank you," she breathed. "Y'all, I have a feeling today is going to be the greatest day of my entire life!"

"So far," Ivy corrected. "The greatest day of your life so far. Leave a little room for improvement in the next four or five decades."

"Yes!" Tally said, clapping her hands enthusiastically. "Oh, I can't believe this. I haven't even seen Audriana and Buster yet—I've got to go find them!"

She leaped to her feet, almost knocking my sandwich out of my hand in the process.

"See y'all at three, okay?" she yelled over her shoulder as she tore wildly off.

I nudged Ivy. "It is kind of amazing, right? I'm so happy for Tally."

"Let's not celebrate the completion of Tally's hopes and dreams just yet," Ivy said. "She could get the flu, too, you know."

"No, she won't," I said, grinning. And I completely believed that. Tally would step into the role of Annie with every cell in her body. And being Annie did not include having the flu—Tally would make sure of that, by sheer force of will.

• • • • • • •

At three on the nose that afternoon, Ivy and I walked into the auditorium. The "actors only" sign had been taken off the door, and nobody objected to our presence. The Drama Club kids were sitting in the first few rows, waiting. The atmosphere was very subdued. I guess people were really worried about what would happen and that the show might get canceled altogether.

Tally was sitting with Buster in the third row.

"Should we just go sit next to her?" I asked Ivy.

She nodded.

We made our way up the aisle and slid into the empty seats.

"Hey, Tally," I said. "Hey, Buster."

Tally turned and smiled at me, but she still looked distinctly nervous. She made a *shh* gesture, putting her finger to her lips, then pointing at her throat.

"Oh no," I said to Buster. "Not again—she was fine at lunch!"

"Nope," Buster said quickly. "No laryngitis. She decided to conserve her voice. If she takes over as Annie, she's going to need every ounce of it, so she's decided to speak only when absolutely necessary."

Tally nodded, confirming Buster's explanation.

"Now *that* I'll have to see to believe," Ivy murmured.

I noticed movement onstage. Mr. Barrymore was walking out from the wings. As usual he looked dignified, even a little elegant, in a black turtleneck and neatly pleated tweed pants.

Buster leaned around Tally and whispered, "Audriana saw him at Foodtown over the weekend. Know what he was getting? Four boxes of Lean Cuisine dinners and a six pack of Tasty-Shack chocolate pudding."

"Thanks, Buster," I said. "Hopefully by the end of the year I can get that image out of my brain."

"I know, right?" Buster asked, grinning. "It's so creepy when you remember your teachers are human."

"Where is Audriana, anyway?" I asked. The three of them always sat together.

Mr. Barrymore cleared his throat loudly. Suddenly every eye in the room was on him, and no one was making a sound.

"Okay," he said. "Let's cut right to the chase. I'm sure you all know that Valerie Teale was sent home with the flu. I spoke to the school nurse, who tells me that in the last three weeks, Valerie is the twenty-eighth student to get this virus. According to her records, the average time students with this strain of the flu have been out is between three and four days. Given that our first complete run-through with costumes and lights is a week from tomorrow, combined with the huge amount of work we need to accomplish in the next several days, I believe the decision is fairly clear-cut. We must recast and have an understudy step in to play Valerie's role."

There was a little murmuring at that. Next to me, Tally said nothing. She sat very still and seemed to be focusing on Mr. Barrymore with every fiber in her body.

"Fortunately, we are professionals. The theater is

full of surprises, and when we are professionals, we find a way to deal with them. Two weeks ago I put out a sign-up sheet for understudies to prepare for just such a surprise. Those of you who signed up were asked to indicate what part you were willing to understudy for. I'm not going to bore you with a long speech about the importance of the understudy—how it often involves a great deal of work with absolutely no payoff—how understudies are literally the unsung heroes of the stage. Suffice it to say . . . not many of you volunteered your names. So I would like to very heartily acknowledge and thank those of you who did."

Mr. Barrymore reached into his pocket and unfolded a piece of paper.

"I've gone over the names of those who signed up to understudy for the part of Annie, reviewed my original audition notes, my rehearsal notes, and had a phone conference with Ms. Whelan, who has, of course, worked with many of you on other productions and has a very good understanding of each of your capabilities as both actors and singers. Taking all of that information into consideration, I have chosen an understudy who I am certain will perform admirably in the role of Annie. So without further ado—our new Annie is Audriana Bingley."

In the brief silence before people began clapping,

I heard Tally's sharp intake of breath. Buster was leaning forward in his seat, looking extremely surprised but clapping. Tally sat frozen, staring straight ahead.

I looked around. Audriana was several rows back. She was sitting up very straight, her expression unreadable. She avoided looking in Tally's direction.

"Okay, we obviously have a lot of work to do to get our new Annie up to speed," Mr. Barrymore was saying. "I'd like to start with a read-through on book, with blocking. So if you are in scene one, bring your script and come up to the stage right now."

Audriana was making her way toward the stage, looking a bit grim, like she was about to go off to war.

"Tal, before you ask, Audie didn't say anything to me about signing up to be an understudy," Buster said.

"Can you blame her?" Ivy asked.

"I'm betting Tally can," Buster said, arching one eyebrow.

I leaned closer to Tally.

"Are you okay?" I asked her.

Tally bit her lower lip, then shook her head. She looked at me, her eyes filled with tears.

"She knew how bad I wanted to get this," Tally said very quietly.

"And she never said anything about wanting the same thing?" I asked.

"Why would she?" Tally snapped. "Audriana doesn't go for the big parts. She's not the leading lady type."

"Well, maybe now she is," Ivy said. "People change. Look at Miko, dumping the PQuit Dance Committee. I'm telling you, I don't think anything would surprise me now."

I squeezed Tally's arm. Now was definitely not the time to point out that this wasn't the first time Tally had classified Audriana as non–leading lady material. That maybe Audriana had taken it to heart and found it hurtful.

"You should talk to her," I said quietly. "Ask her why she didn't tell you."

Tally fixed me with a look I'd never seen from her before. It was angry and cold.

"I am never, ever speaking to Audriana Bingley again," Tally said grimly.

I heard the pianist begin playing the first song. The actors had taken their places onstage. Mr. Barrymore was still there, leading Audriana to the spot where Annie was supposed to be standing. He was pointing to the script she held and explaining something. Audriana listened intently, nodding every once in a while. Mr. Barrymore gave a satisfied nod and hopped off the stage, standing at seat level with his arms folded as the read-through began.

I snuck another look at Tally. Her expression was still angry, but this time her eyes were not on Audriana.

She was staring at Mr. Barrymore, her lips pressed tightly together.

Onstage, Audriana began to sing.

· chapter ·
18

"Okay, so what's this big thing you have to tell me?" I asked when Ivy came into my room and closed the door behind her.

"It's news. I talked to my parents last night, just like I promised. I asked them to tell me flat out what was going on, and they did. There's good news and bad news. Which do you want first?"

Oh no. I didn't want to find out what day Ivy was moving. I especially didn't want to find that out right now as I was getting ready for one of the biggest nights of my life. But if she wanted to talk about it . . . then I guess we would talk about it.

"Um, bad news first, I guess," I said. Might as well get it over with.

"The bad news is that the publishing director of *4 Girls*—that would be me—is a world-class Olympic-level moron."

"Um . . . okay . . . not sure I agree with that, but am I supposed to ask for the good news now?"

"Yep," Ivy said. "The good news is . . . drumroll, please . . . we are not moving!"

My mouth dropped open.

"*WHAT?!*" I shrieked.

Ivy nodded, laughing. "I'm staying! We're not going anywhere!"

I lunged to hug Ivy, remembering just in time to turn my face away so I didn't smear the moisturizer I had slathered on all over her beautiful dress.

"What happened?" I cried. "She didn't take the job?"

"She *did* take the job," Ivy said. "She's working from home—it was never supposed to be an office job. *City Nation* wants her as an editorial consultant. She'll have to go in to their office a few times a month, but that's it! That's why they never told me—there was nothing to tell, at least there was only the job thing, and they were still fiddling with the details."

"You're not moving! Woot!!"

"Right?" Ivy asked with a wild grin on her face. "And that's what I get for eavesdropping. With my ear pressed up against the door, I only got half the story. You were *soooo* right when you tried to convince me to just talk to my mother. If I'd just asked her what was going on, I would have known there was never any discussion of moving. I basically invented that entire drama in my own head!"

"It's because you hang around Tally more now," I said. "It's contagious."

"We better hope that's not true," Ivy said. She made one final adjustment to my necklace.

"You're not moving," I said, because it sounded so fabulous to say.

"I am *not* moving," Ivy repeated. "Now sit down—I want to fix your hair."

The heavy feeling I'd been carrying around—that this great thing I had been given was being taken away—disappeared. I felt fabulous.

"This is so amazing. I can't wait to tell Evelyn. Hey, speaking of Tally, you haven't heard from her, have you?" I asked Ivy, who was now doing something to my hair as I sat patiently on the edge of my bed. "I mean, outside of seeing her in class, obviously."

"Not since the understudy thing on Wednesday," Ivy said, frowning as she concentrated on whatever she was doing to the back of my head.

"Me neither," I told her. "She hasn't responded to any of my e-mails. It's been three days. I'm worried about her."

"I know," Ivy said. "But I don't think there's anything we can do for her right now. She's got to get through this. She's furious at her best friend, and she feels humiliated that she didn't get the part. Plus, remember, she practically idolized Mr. Barrymore, only to find out he wasn't exactly the guy she thought he was. That's a lot."

"It is a lot," I said. "That's why I'm worried about her."

"Well, for now," Ivy said, standing back to admire her handiwork, "let's just worry about you and this dance. Your hair looks good. It's going to be time to go soon."

I felt a flutter in my stomach as I got up to check my reflection.

"And you really think it's better to wear my hair down?" I asked nervously, examining my reflection in the full-length mirror on my closet door. Ivy had made little braids and connected them with a sparkly clip in the back, but the rest hung loose.

"Definitely," Ivy said. "These curls are amazing. And boys love long hair. Paulina, look at yourself!"

I was. The hair, the dress, the boots Ivy had lent me—everything was working.

I look really pretty, I thought.

"Now all you need is some perfume," Ivy said.

"Oh no, Ivy, I never wear perfume," I said quickly. "I don't like the way any of it smells."

"You'll like this," Ivy said, pulling a little glass bottle out of her purse. "It's called Japanese

177

Agarwood. Lisa Hoffman makes it, and all of her stuff is amazing."

She opened the little bottle and let me smell it. It was wonderful. A mix of flower and wood and a hint of spice.

"I love it," I said. Because I really did.

Ivy applied a few dabs to my neck and wrist.

"Just enough," she said. "The trick to perfume is to never put too much of it on. Paulie, you look absolutely gorgeous."

I gave Ivy a tight hug.

"You look gorgeous, too," I said.

Ivy grinned and did a little spin. She was wearing an emerald-green, silk dress with tiny, pink flowers embroidered on it.

"Vintage," she said. "It's from China."

"It's amazing," I said. "Listen, are you sure you don't want to ride over with us?"

"Are you nuts?" Ivy said. "I'm not hitching a ride along on your first date. I'll see you over there. I'll be the one standing at the punch bowl pretending not to watch you."

There was a knock on my door, which swung open before I had a chance to respond.

My mother stood there staring at me. She began to shake her head, looking slightly dazed. I felt suddenly alarmed.

"What?" I asked. "Why are you doing that?"

Then I noticed her eyes filling with tears. She waved her hand in front of her face—the old a-breeze-will-help-me-stop-being-emotional gesture, and she smiled.

"Sweetie, you just look *so* . . . beautiful," she said, her voice quavering.

I blushed.

"Mom, stop," I murmured. She was embarrassing me. But it was also kind of nice.

Kevin appeared in the doorway behind my mother, and when he saw me, he looked like he was gearing up to utter the loudest laugh he could muster. But when he caught sight of Ivy standing behind me, he clamped his mouth shut, his face turning bright red. I no longer had any doubt. The kid was *totally* crushing on my best friend.

"Heya, squirt," Ivy addressed him. "Keeping the battlestar clean and the universe free of Cylons?"

"No," Kevin said. He dashed out of the room. "I mean, yes!" he yelled over his shoulder.

My mother smiled.

"Ivy, did you say your mother is picking you up at six fifteen?" she asked.

Ivy nodded.

"Okay. That's in just a few minutes—I'll leave you two alone."

She closed the door. I took a big breath and grinned like an idiot at Ivy.

"Benny is coming here at seven," I said. "I'm so afraid I'm going to make a fool of myself."

"You are not," Ivy said. "Stop saying that or you will hypnotize yourself into actually acting like a fool!"

I laughed. "I feel hypnotized. Like I'm sleepwalking. I'll probably forget something really obvious and important, like my shoes."

I heard voices downstairs.

"Sounds like my mom's here to pick me up," Ivy said. "So I'll see you at the dance in, like, an hour, okay?"

I gulped. "Okay."

"It's going to be an amazing night, Paulie," Ivy promised as she walked out of my room.

I had awakened that morning knowing it was going to be an amazing night. With Ivy's news, it had just gone from amazing to perfect.

· chapter ·
19

A car pulled up outside my house at exactly seven. When I opened the front door, Benny did kind of a double take. I guess because he'd never seen me all dressed up before. I took it as a compliment. He cleaned up very nicely himself. His usual varsity jacket or grass-stained lacrosse uniform was replaced with neatly pressed khaki pants, a deep-blue oxford shirt with the sleeves rolled up, and a paisley tie. Frankly, I thought he looked like a movie star. We smiled at the same time, and I felt like the sun had just come out and a beam was shining right on me.

From everything I'd ever heard about A First Date, there was supposed to be plenty of Awkward, particularly if your mother was driving you to your destination. But this was the exact opposite. Benny chatted easily with my mother. He talked about school and how guys totally read *4 Girls* but they just didn't admit it, why he planned to make his own lacrosse stick from twigs and twine just to see if he could, and how he'd seen a woman at Foodtown pushing a stroller so enormous it blocked the entire aisle and what did we bet that child would grow into an adult who would one day drive a Hummer.

"I mean, if you get used to that much personal space when you're still a toddler," Benny said, "it can only go downhill from there."

My mother laughed. "Very astute observation," she said. "Okay—here we are. I'll be back to pick you up at nine thirty."

"Thanks, Mom," I said, getting out of the car.

Once again, I figured I was due for a hefty dose of Awkward. But Benny walked me into that dance like it was the most normal thing in the world. I was aware of people looking over and checking us out. But Benny made me feel so completely at ease I didn't care who was watching. Actually, I felt really proud to be seen with him.

"Wow, check this place out," Benny exclaimed.

The gym looked great. I had to hand it to Shelby and the Dance Committee. Each wall was dedicated to a decade. I can't imagine where they got all the stuff, from pictures of all The Beatles and hippie beads on the sixties wall to Madonna album covers and a huge movie poster of *Back to the Future* on the eighties wall. They'd even organized a DJ to switch decades every song. We were currently in the seventies, as evidence by the huge number of people singing and dancing to "YMCA." When Michael Jackson's "Thriller" signaled we had moved into the eighties, Benny touched my arm.

"We cannot *not* dance to this song!" he yelled over the music.

"I agree!" I yelled back.

We ended up being able to not *NOT* dance through two entire decade cycles. I was starting to worry that my hair was getting stuck to my face and my carefully applied makeup was migrating toward my chin.

"Gonna run to the girls' room!" I shouted, but the music ended just as the words "girls' room" left my mouth and echoed around the large room.

"Gotcha," Benny said.

He certainly did. Everyone heard and was once again staring. *Oh well,* I thought.

Ivy was standing by the water fountain chatting with an eighth-grade guy I didn't really know. I caught her eye and nodded my head toward the locker room.

The air in the locker room was cool, and the sound of the blaring music became more muffled when the door swung closed. Then it opened again.

"I don't even need to ask you how it's going," Ivy said. "You guys look like you're having a blast out there. The boy can dance!"

I couldn't help myself—I grinned wildly.

"However, we need to do something about your hair," Ivy added, pulling a comb out of her purse.

My smile faded. "Is it bad?"

"Yes," Ivy said matter-of-factly. "Come here."

"Ow," I said as she started carefully combing the hair back from my face.

"Stand still," Ivy instructed. "So I've already gotten some great shots of the dance for us to use in the magazine. We've got everything else, Tally's still okay with us printing the interview, and that means once you write the review of *Annie*, we're almost done!"

"Yep. You're coming to the dress rehearsal with me Thursday, right? I'll go home and write the whole thing that night so we can get the disk to the printer Friday before school. We'll have copies to hand out on Monday morning—right on schedule!"

"Perfect. We're the dynamic duo, you and me. Okay, I'm done," Ivy said, putting the comb away. "You're as good as new. Now you'd better get back out there and find your boyfriend."

"Ivy!" I objected, giving her a little shove. I checked my reflection one last time in the mirror. "It's one date. He's not my boyfriend."

"Not yet," Ivy corrected. She checked her watch. "But the night is still young!"

I'm the last person who would know how this stuff gets decided—when friends become more than friends, or at what moment it becomes understood that you've gone from having a date to having a boyfriend. I'm totally clueless.

But I had a feeling that when it came down to it, I would just know. And that it would be the same as Benny asking me out—the same as the drive over in the car.

Easy. Fun. And totally natural.

· chapter ·
20

Even though I'd only been an observer to all the work that went into *Annie*, the energy was contagious. It wasn't opening night, but it was the first time the actors would run through the entire showcase with their lines memorized, with lights and costumes and no breaks no matter what went wrong. And there would be other people in the audience. Mr. Barrymore called it an "invited dress rehearsal." So it was kind of a big deal, and I felt as nervous and excited as if I were going up on the stage myself.

To my surprise, Miko had agreed to join me and Ivy for the performance. Because Kevin had a karate demonstration that night, my mother dropped me off at the school a little early, and I went to the green room, which was really just the French classroom, to hang out with the actors. I really wanted to see Tally. Through the whole long week since Annie had been recast, it was like the light had just gone out of her. And I knew from Buster that she had not spoken a word to Audriana. Buster said both of them were miserable. Buster, however, remained his usual exuberant self, dancing in and out of the doorway when I arrived.

"Another opening, another show," he sang in a lovely tenor voice. "Da da dada, ta tee ta taaaaaaah, another opening of another show. Hey, Paulie!"

He danced back through the doorway, and I followed him into the classroom. It looked like most of the cast was already there. Tally was standing in front of a mirror—one of many that had been set up in the back of the room. She was applying some powder to her face and checking her reflection.

"Hi, Buster," I said. "So are you ready?"

"Always," he declared.

"How about Audriana?"

Buster's expression grew more serious.

"She's not here yet," he said. "She's really nervous, though, I can tell you that."

"But it's only the dress rehearsal," I said. "She's got time."

"Try telling her that," Buster said. "We had a stop and start yesterday—that's when we run through the showcase, but we're allowed to break if we need to, and she forgot her lines a bunch of times and missed an entrance on one of her biggest songs. She's really rattled."

"I'm going to go talk to Tal. Hey, has she made up with Audriana yet?"

"Nope. I think at this point she actually really wants to," Buster said. "She just wants it all to be behind them. But Tally is really stubborn, and she still feels like Audriana should have told her she put herself on that understudy list, which I have to say I agree with. Tally's sorry, but she doesn't want to say so first. So she goes on refusing to talk to Audriana at all. I think that's part of the problem for Audie. It's hard enough stepping up to be a leading lady like that, but when you know your best friend thinks you basically stole the part from her, well . . . all the worse."

"Well, at least you're speaking to both of them," I said. "Poor Audriana. And Tally's not mad at you for not taking sides? How are you managing that?"

"I'm Switzerland," Buster sang, tossing his hat in the air and ducking under it so it landed right on his head.

"Nice move," said Mr. Barrymore as he came through the door.

"Oh, you're too kind," Buster said, bowing. "No applause, please, folks. Just money!"

"Okay, everybody, I'm going to make this brief," Mr. Barrymore said.

I scooched into a seat nearby.

"First of all, please make sure you've all signed in with Dana, our wonderful stage manager, so that I know you're all here," he said. "Remember, we do everything tonight as we will on opening night. For all practical purposes, this is a real performance."

At that moment Audriana came through the door. She looked as white as a ghost. She sat down on top of a bookcase just inside the door and looked at the ground, her arms folded tightly over her stomach.

"Great. Now we're here to relax, to warm up, to check last-minute notes, whatever it is that you need. As you can see, there is hot tea, lemon, and plenty of water available on the table in the back—please help yourselves. We have a half hour until Dana will call places. Everyone who is working on this showcase is a member of this family, and this is our time to relax and to be there for each other. Remember, there are no small parts—only small actors. Each and every one of you is a huge star."

People started clapping. A number of "orphans" stood up and bowed.

"As you know, the theater is full of superstitions, and one of them is that it is bad luck to wish a person good luck before a performance. So let's all go with the traditional words—break a leg!"

"Break a leg!" came the shouted response.

Mr. Barrymore clapped. Then the actors clapped. Realizing Mr. Barrymore was done talking, I hurried over to Tally and gave her a hug.

"Hey," I said. "So break a leg!"

Tally brightened when she saw me.

"You're here! Y'all break a leg, too."

"Are you okay?" I asked, sitting down on the window ledge so I was closer to eye level with her.

"I'm usually a basket case during final dress," Tally replied. "But being in the orphan chorus, there's really not that many ways I can mess up. It's actually kind of refreshing to not be so stressed out over lines and stuff—I'm really going to get to enjoy myself tonight."

"That's great, Tal!" I said.

"I wish Buster would stop dancing around like that, though," Tally began. "He always . . ."

Her voice trailed off midsentence, her eyes on the door. A stout, white-haired man was standing in the doorway. When Mr. Barrymore saw him, he waved and walked quickly over to greet him.

"I wonder if that's him," she said.

"Him who?"

Tally looked at me as if I'd said I'd never heard of chocolate.

"The secret agent!" she said. "I never did find a picture—I sort of forgot about it after the Kansas thing. Come on, let's go spy a little."

I wasn't too keen on spying, but Tally had already jumped up and was heading for the door. I followed her.

Mr. Barrymore and the white-haired man were walking down the hall and chatting. Tally pretended to take a drink at the water fountain, then fake-fussed with her shoelace, trying to decide what to do. Just then, Audriana walked into the hall. Tally caught sight of her, then looked away.

Audriana looked like she wanted to say something. Instead, she took a deep breath, then bent over, her hands on her knees. She looked like she was about to faint.

"Audriana? Are you okay?" I asked.

She looked up at me, then at Tally. She shook her head.

"I don't know. I'm not sure I can do this."

"Of course, you can," I assured her, sneaking a sidelong glance at Tally, who appeared to be fixing a button on the front of her costume. "You'll be fine. And it's only a dress rehearsal."

"It's the same as a performance—there's an audience," Tally reminded me.

Audriana stood up. Her face had gone from white to green.

"I don't think I can pull this off," she said. "All the lines, the songs . . ."

I shot Tally a pleading look, but she just fussed with the button.

"Audriana, you can. You can do this," I said firmly.

Audriana shook her head again.

"I can't," she said weakly. "I'm not like Tally. It's like she said, some of us are leading ladies, and some of us aren't."

Tally froze. I could see from her face that she remembered saying just that. Now she was seeing the effect one badly thought-out remark had on her best friend.

"That isn't true," Tally said suddenly. "Audie, that was a ridiculous thing that I said about leading ladies. It was stupid and petty, and I never should have said it, and I certainly didn't mean it. Mr. Barrymore picked you to take over *Annie* for a reason, Aud. Because you are a leading lady. He knows it, Ms. Whelan knows it, and I know it better than anybody else. We're both leading lady material—but this is your show. It's your time. And you're going to be amazing tonight. Now you look me in the eye and tell me you can do this."

Audriana raised her head and locked eyes with Tally.

"Tal . . . I am so sorry about—"

Tally shushed her.

"Say it," she commanded.

Audriana took a deep breath.

"I can do this," she said.

"That's what I'm talking about, y'all!" Tally declared. "Now what are you doing standing out here? Come on. You've got to drink some hot tea and do your warm-ups. Maybe run the lines for the first scene—I'll help you."

Tally pulled Audriana by the arm, leading her back into the classroom.

I stood by myself for a moment, feeling like I'd just survived a tornado.

Then I followed my friends inside.

· chapter ·
21

When the lights came up onstage, the small audience fell silent. A single spotlight came up on Audriana, dressed in rags and standing in the center of the stage, the forms of sleeping orphans dimly visible in the background. The familiar opening bars of "Maybe" began.

But Audriana missed her entrance to the song. The pianist repeated the opening bars, and my heart started pounding. Was Audriana freezing up? I thought I saw a hint of panic creeping onto her face. She missed her entrance a second time, and the pianist played the opening chords a third time. I saw movement behind Audriana—an orphan with wild, curly, blond hair sitting up in bed, yawning, and offering Annie a teddy bear and a sweet smile.

I don't think that bit was in the script. But it did the trick.

Audriana took the bear, and when her third chance came, she opened her mouth and began to sing. She was pitch-perfect, and she didn't miss a beat after that for the rest of the show.

I should have known that in the end, Tally would be there for Audriana.

She was certifiably nuts and impossibly spacey, but loyal to the end. As far as I was concerned, Tally was a leading lady all the way.

Audriana had really pulled it off. The performance was certainly not perfect. Miss Hannigan tripped over Rooster Cogburn's foot and fell flat on her face. Daddy Warbucks skipped an entire section of lines, and everyone had to scramble and improvise. At one point, all the lights went out for a moment, then blinked back on a second later. Definitely not perfect. But Mr. Barrymore looked very happy. He asked the cast to meet him back in the green room for notes afterward. Ivy, Miko, and I tagged along and listened quietly while Mr. Barrymore ran through his list of notes for the actors. And it was a long list. Finally he put his notebook down.

"You have been through a lot this last week," Mr. Barrymore told his cast. "You all have the equivalent of two full-time jobs—your classes and schoolwork are a full-time commitment, and you've been working as hard as you can on this show on top of that. Then our Annie comes down with the flu, and we must have an understudy step in. Let me tell you, people, professional shows have folded under less duress than this. I am very proud of all of you. I'm proud of you, Audriana, for taking over the part so wonderfully when we all know how much extra work it meant for you. And I'm proud of you, Valerie, for coming back on Tuesday and being willing to take a part in the chorus. That is *true* professionalism. You should both be congratulating yourselves, and as for the rest of the cast, well done. You really hit one out of the park tonight."

Everyone clapped and hollered, and with Mr. Barrymore's words, even I felt a glow of accomplishment, though I was only here to report my findings. I decided to stay long enough to get a piece of the cake I'd seen being unwrapped on the refreshment table before heading home to write my review.

Valerie had been following the white-haired man around, talking to him nonstop about her voice coach and her plans to go to Yale School of Drama. To my surprise, Tally wasn't at all bothered by the fact that Valerie had found out about the secret agent and was commandeering him—she was too busy competing with Buster to see who could get a bigger bite of cake into their mouth and clowning around with Audriana. But when Mr. Barrymore stood up again to say he wanted to introduce the whole cast to someone very special, Tally momentarily stopped flying around the room to listen. It appeared the revelation of the secret agent was finally at hand.

"He's come all the way from Kansas to see the show. He's very important to me, and I can honestly say that if it were not for him, I wouldn't be here. So, all of you, please give a big welcome to my dad!"

Tally stifled a giggle by slapping her hand over her mouth.

"His dad?" I asked.

"I guess he's not the secret agent," Tally squealed. Buster was almost bent double from laughing.

"Oh, you guys, Valerie has been following him around all night trying to impress him and he's Mr. Barrymore's dad!" Buster wheezed.

"Will you please look at Valerie's expression right now?" Audriana whispered loudly. "She looks so mad I think I actually see steam coming out of her ears!"

Tally clutched Audriana so that she wouldn't collapse from laughing.

I laughed, too. But I also had a bit of respect for Valerie now. She had rubbed everybody's noses in it when she got the lead, but in the end she was not too proud to come back and take a tiny part in the chorus. That said something about the girl as far as I was concerned.

Ivy and Miko, who were sitting together near the back of the room, were watching us curiously.

"What is so funny?" Ivy mouthed.

I grinned and went over to fill them in on every detail. It was one of the best moments of the night. And like most really great nights, it was over in a flash.

· chapter ·

22

Annie—The Review

Students and parents of Bixby Middle School are in for a rare treat—a Drama Club showcase of Annie, where the leading ladies and gents of the Drama Club will perform the most memorable scenes and songs from the show. You've read about the behind-the-scenes work that everyone has been pouring into the show right here in 4 Girls. But what can you expect from the production? This reporter was lucky enough to attend a special dress rehearsal performance.

From the moment the curtain went up, I was captivated. A two-story set with sliding flats makes a magical transformation from orphanage to city town house. The costumes are eye-catching, and the musical accompaniment had me tapping my toes. But the real wow factor here is the cast themselves. There were times when I had to remind myself that these weren't professional actors, they were kids— some of them friends of mine! From the dance numbers to the powerhouse musical solos, from the trials of the orphanage to the extravagant luxury of Daddy Warbucks's town house, it was all mesmerizing and a team effort all the way.

Two people deserve special mention. Valerie Teale was originally cast as Annie. I sat in on her audition and some of the early rehearsals. She was amazing. She knows her stuff, and she sings so beautifully you'd swear she was a pro. Unfortunately, Valerie had to drop the lead when she got the dreaded Bixby flu. With barely a week to go, Audriana Bingley was handpicked to take over the part. Audriana knocked herself out getting the lines and blocking down in record time, but when you see her, you won't be able to believe she stepped in at the last minute. She absolutely shines onstage. If Valerie and Audriana both end up on Broadway, I'll be the first in line to buy tickets.

Special credit is due to another person who had to step in unexpectedly. Gideon Barrymore is a professional actor who has appeared in a variety of productions onstage and on-screen. You can learn more about him by reading the interview he gave Tally Janeway on p. 2. This wonderful, rich production could not have come together without its director. This reporter, for one, is grateful he came to Bixby to run the show.

Don't wait to buy your tickets and see this show—you can trust me when I tell you that the Drama Club really knocks this one out of the park!

• • • • • • •

The cafeteria was always loud and rowdy. But today the volume seemed especially amped up.

And this time, Tally was not to blame. Not directly, anyway. I guess you could say she was one-fourth responsible.

This Monday was all about *4 Girls*. Ivy, Tally, and I had carried the boxes of printed magazines to school early and passed them out to everyone who wanted one when the first lunch bell rang. Judging from the reaction in the cafeteria, people were happy with what they saw. I stood in the doorway a moment, listening to all the comments that floated by.

"There's Cara. Cara—did you see this picture of you?"

"Ha, it says, 'The groovy, hipster, tie-dyed eighth-graders'! Dude, we're groovy!"

"Hey, according to this Barrymore guy, I need TV shows and movies to release my deepest fears and to channel the collective unconscious of myths and legends! Channel me, people!"

"Okay, like, which seventy-eight percent of girls are terrified of insects? Because I'm not!"

"I cannot believe I wore that!"

It was good. People seemed happy. But I didn't want to get pulled into the cafeteria because Miko had texted us all last night to ask if we could meet at the picnic table outside. As much as I wanted to go into the cafeteria and bask in the attention, I was more interested in knowing why Miko wanted us to meet. I went into the hallway in the direction of the side door.

"Paulina," I heard.

Shelby had come up behind me, holding the magazine in her hands.

"Hi," I said. "I'm kind of supposed to be somewhere right now."

"That's fine," Shelby said as if I had been asking for permission. "I just wanted to say that you really should have used my idea to focus on just the seventh grade for this article. It would have been much better. We had more spirit than the eighth-graders by dressing up two days in a row. And Homecoming and

4 Girls are all about school spirit."

I smiled.

"Well, maybe you're right," I said. "I guess we'll never know."

"No, we never will," Shelby said, flipping her hair out of her face.

I started to go, but she stopped me.

"I did like this part, though," she said, pointing at one of the photographs I'd chosen.

The picture was of the PQuits the day before Decade Day. I remembered very clearly the moment when Norah took it. They were standing by the lockers in their outlandish seventies getups. Miko and Shelby stood in the center of the group, their arms around each other, flanked by the others. Shelby towered over her friends in her crazy platform shoes. Miko looked gorgeous in her white suit and was beaming from ear to ear for the camera. The caption below the picture read:

The decade that arrived early! The eighth grade may have won the School Spirit Award for their hippie costumes, but we can't deny the incredible showing by the seventh-graders who were so full of spirit they ushered the seventies in a little ahead of schedule! Kudos to all of them—outrageous and unique as always!

"Glad you liked it," I said.

I was secretly relieved. It had been a bit of a gamble to include a photo of what might be considered one of Shelby Simpson's most embarrassing moments. But Miko had turned it into fun, and the photograph showed a bunch of PQuits at the center of everyone's attention having a good time.

"Yeah," Shelby said. "And we totally should have won for our bringing the decade early idea. Anyway. Whatever."

I grinned.

"Whatever," I repeated.

Miko, Ivy, and Tally were already at the bench when I got there. They each still had the copies of *4 Girls* I had given them before lunch.

"It really does look amazing," Miko said. "You guys did so well."

"Thanks," I replied, sitting down next to her. "It's not quite as good as the first one—there's just a little something missing. A little . . . splash."

Miko smiled.

"Thanks, I think," she said.

"And the review is perfect!" Tally exclaimed. "But, oh my gosh, what if Audriana hadn't started singing? What if she had completely tanked and run offstage— would you have put that in the review?"

"Let's not even think about that," Ivy said. "People

love this interview, Tal. Seriously, it might not have as much 'splash' as the first issue, but I think we did a fabulous job."

"You did," Miko said. "You all did. It's perfect."

"Not quite," I said. "We need you back, Miko. If we're going to get it perfect the next time, we need The Four to really be The Four again. Forever, this time. We need you, Miko."

I had a whole speech prepared. I'd thought about it over and over again—I knew all the perfect things to say so Miko would have absolutely no choice but to realize I was right, and she should come back. But Miko interrupted me before I could even get started.

"I would love to," she said. "If you still want me, then I'm back in one hundred percent."

"Miko, I knew it!" I exclaimed. "I knew you'd come back, I was positive. I am so happy."

"We all are," Ivy said. "Paulina's right—it takes all four of us to get the magic right. I'm really glad you decided to stay."

"Thanks," Miko said. She was beaming. "So you guys probably already have a plan for the next issue, I'm guessing. Which is fine—just tell me what you need done, and I'm on it."

Ivy and I looked at each other.

"Actually, we haven't talked at all about the next issue," I said. "I guess we better get cracking."

"Everyone promise to go home and think tonight, and we'll have a mini-meeting at lunch tomorrow," Ivy said. "But for now, let's go back into the cafeteria. The whole school is talking about *4 Girls*. By tonight, they'll be talking about something else. Let's go enjoy it while it lasts!"

· chapter ·
23

"I'm dying," Kevin wailed, curled miserably in his bed. "I think some of my fingers are falling off!"

Kevin had finally achieved his dream—he had come down with the dreaded Bixby flu.

Unfortunately, he'd made it through the entire school week and had woken up sick on Saturday morning.

"Do you want to play Sonic the Hedgehog with me?"

I usually never let Kevin anywhere near my laptop because he always managed to get the keyboard sticky.

"My eyeballs can't take it," he complained. "I think they're swelling up. I'm pretty sure they're going to pop right out of my head. I can't do anything! How did I get this stupid flu, anyway?"

I could think of about five ways, but I was much

too nice a sister to point them out.

The doorbell rang.

"I wonder who that is?" I asked. "We're not expecting anybody."

"It's probably the fundertakers," Kevin groaned. "Because they know I'm about to die, and they're going to take me away to the funder parlor to bury me in the graveyard."

I stood up.

"I'm going to go see," I told him. "Try to get some sleep, buddy. You'll feel better in a while, I promise."

I walked downstairs and opened the front door just enough to peek out.

"Wow! What are you guys doing here?" I exclaimed.

Ivy, Miko, and Tally were standing together on the front doorstep.

"I knew you were sticking close to home to help out with Kevin," Ivy said. "So we thought we'd pop by and surprise you. Is it okay?"

"Sure," I said, delighted. I opened the door all the way to let them in. "Kevin's upstairs dying, so if you hear screams of agony, don't be alarmed. Mom had to run out to pick up some groceries. Hopefully she'll be back soon."

"We can't stay too long," Ivy said. "Miko's dad is coming back in a few minutes. He's just running an errand."

"Okay," I said, confused.

My friends trooped into the living room and sat down in various comfy spots around the room.

"Something's come up, and I wanted to tell you all about it at the same time, in person," Ivy said.

"If you tell me you actually are moving I'm going to jump out the window," I said.

Ivy laughed.

"Sorry, you're stuck with me," she said. "Here's the thing—I know we came up with an outline for issue number three this week, and if you guys want to stick with that, it's fine."

"But . . . ," Miko prompted.

"But." Ivy took a deep breath. "My mom went into the city to meet with the people she's going to work with at *City Nation*. She happened to bring a copy of *4 Girls* along with her."

"*City Nation* magazine saw our magazine?" Tally asked, a little breathlessly. "Wow!"

"That isn't even the best part," Ivy said. "Okay, some of the editors took a look, and of course they loved it because it's a fabulous magazine. And . . . they made a little offer."

"A little offer?" Miko asked.

"An invitation," Ivy said. "The four of us are invited on an all-expenses-paid trip to New York City for three days over Thanksgiving break to work on a special joint issue with their editors. Their work will appear in the next *4 Girls* issue, and our work will be in the Christmas edition of *City Nation*!"

Tally screamed.

"*City Nation* is like a huge national magazine," Miko said. "Practically half the country reads it!"

"And we'd be in it?" I asked.

"They want to interview us, write about us, and publish some of our original *4 Girls* content," Ivy said. "And they'll pay for everything—meals, hotel, the works."

"I'm going to faint," Tally announced.

"Ivy . . . this is unbelievable!" I said.

"Do you guys think your parents will be okay with letting you go?" Ivy asked. "My mom will be there as a chaperone. It's three nights."

"I know I'll be able to go," Tally said. "And my sister is going to be *sooooo* jealous!"

"Miko?" Ivy asked.

"My parents might take some convincing," Miko said. "But don't worry. They *will* end up giving me permission."

"We're going to New York City!" I said, amazed. I couldn't wait to ask my mom.

"We're going to be famous!" Tally added.

"We're going to have to work really hard," Ivy cautioned.

"And we're going to have a blast," Miko added.

It was all true and, boy, was there a lot to think about. And a lot to do. Getting stuff ready for the middle school to read was hard enough. Now we would be writing and creating things that thousands of people would see. Tens of thousands!

As Ivy told us all about *City Nation* and the places we'd get to see in NYC, I felt a sudden lurch of panic in my stomach, like Audriana must have felt when the spotlight came up on her at the opening of *Annie*. Was I good enough to take on such a big responsibility? Would my writing, even my ideas, seem small and silly when they were printed in a copy of the great *City Nation*? Could I do this?

But all at once, the panicked feeling disappeared.

I don't have to do anything, I thought. *It isn't me. It's US.*

The Four.

Suddenly Miko stood up. "My dad's back, guys," she said. "We should probably get going."

"I'll walk you out," I said, standing and following my friends to the door.

Ivy paused on the front step while Miko and Tally got into the car. "Can you believe this, Paulie?"

"I can't," I said, a little breathless. I couldn't believe everything that had happened in the last week, and yet it had *all* happened. I felt like a million bucks.

Ivy gave me a quick hug and then bounded down the steps and into the car. I watched as Miko's dad pulled out of the driveway. As he turned up the street, the license plate caught my eye: GALILEA7

"What?" I muttered. That was the name of one of the blogposters . . . the one who . . .

And suddenly everything made sense. I smiled. Miko had never *really* left us after all. Now I felt like a million and one.

We'd always been four, but now we were officially back together—and not a moment too soon. We had our magic back.

And I had a feeling that when we got to New York City, we were going to need every single bit of it.

Because as everybody knows, anything can happen in New York.

ABOUT THE AUTHOR

Elizabeth Cody Kimmel is a widely published author of thirty books for children and young adults, including *The Reinvention of Moxie Roosevelt* and the *Suddenly Supernatural* and *Lily B.* series. Elizabeth is proud to admit that she was never asked to sit at the Prom-Queens-in-Training table at her middle-school cafeteria. She likes reading, hiking, peanut butter cups, and *Star Trek*, but not at the same time. You can visit her at www.codykimmel.com.